"Don't y   ne?"

"What?" D

Alys

Still

with   point.

"Never mind," he murmured. "I can feel it."

He was right. Her heart was racing like mad. And she wanted him, no matter how wrong it was.

"I'm such a fool," she said.

"Why?"

"I believed everything you told me before, and here I am believing you all over again." From the first moment Derek had caught her eye, she'd had the feeling he could read her every thought.

"I haven't lied to you. Not this time," he murmured, edging closer to her.

"No lies, maybe. Just a few gaping omissions."

"You can believe this," he said, slipping his arm around her waist. "Not a day has gone by in the last six months that I haven't wanted you."

With that, he dragged her to him and kissed her.

Dear Reader,

What if you had a scorching one-week affair with a sexy, mysterious man, only to have him disappear without a trace? What if you found out every word he'd told you during that week was a lie, including his real name? What if fate brought you face-to-face with him again six months later in a luxury high-rise apartment penthouse, and he appeared to be *robbing* the place?

In *One Night in Texas,* this is the situation Alyssa Ballard finds herself in. But during the next twenty-four hours she discovers the secret behind the man she was once so infatuated with, and suddenly she's falling for him all over again.

I love to create stories where my characters end up together through unusual circumstances neither one of them could have anticipated. I hope you enjoy *One Night in Texas,* and that it holds a few surprises for you, too.

Visit my Web site at www.janesullivan.com, or write to me at jane@janesullivan.com. I'd love to hear from you!

Best wishes,

Jane Sullivan

Books by Jane Sullivan

HARLEQUIN TEMPTATION
854—ONE HOT TEXAN
898—RISKY BUSINESS
960—TALL, DARK AND TEXAN
1002—WHEN HE WAS BAD...

HARLEQUIN DUETS
33—STRAY HEARTS
48—THE MATCHMAKER'S MISTAKE

JANE SULLIVAN

ONE NIGHT IN TEXAS

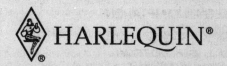

TORONTO • NEW YORK • LONDON
AMSTERDAM • PARIS • SYDNEY • HAMBURG
STOCKHOLM • ATHENS • TOKYO • MILAN • MADRID
PRAGUE • WARSAW • BUDAPEST • AUCKLAND

This book is dedicated to the people who have read my
Harlequin Temptation novels over the years, with
special thanks to those of you who have written to me
with such kind words or shared my books with
other readers. I hope you enjoy this one!

ISBN 0-373-69222-6

ONE NIGHT IN TEXAS

Copyright © 2005 by Jane Graves.

1

He sat alone at the bar, a darkly handsome man surrounded by an aura of mystery that made the very air around him quiver with tension. Underdressed for the trendy Seattle hotel club, he wore a pair of jeans and a fitted black T-shirt, but after one look at those eyes, not a soul would have suggested he adhere to a dress code.

At least fifteen minutes had passed since the drink in front of him had touched his lips. He paid no attention to the lively atmosphere in the club. Ignored the bartender when he spoke to him. Barely moved a muscle.

He only had eyes for her.

Sitting at a nearby table, she felt the power of his presence like a knockout punch. No matter how many times she looked away, when she glanced back, his gaze was still fixed on her, his eyes like daggers that could rip right through the fabric of her dress and leave her completely naked.

The game continued between them for several more minutes. At his unrelenting attention, her cheeks flushed and her skin grew taut and prickly.

He wanted her. She knew it. They'd never exchanged a word, yet still she knew it.

Then, inexplicably, he turned away. Rising from the bar, he tossed down a bill and then headed for the door of the club.

Disappointment surged through her. She told herself it was for the best, that she had no business messing with a man who exuded danger, but the sexual tension he radiated still made fantasies spring to her mind.

But as he neared the door, he slowed down. Stopped. Turning around, he met her eyes again.

And waited.

But even as he issued the invitation, his eyes flashed a warning. He was telling her that if she gave in to temptation, she did so at her own risk.

Some unfathomable force drove her to stand. Saying nothing to her friends, she sidestepped the table and walked toward the doorway, as if an invisible thread were drawing her to him.

Even if she was having second thoughts, he didn't give her the chance to reconsider. Without a word, he took her by the hand and headed for the elevators, forcing her to keep up with his long, purposeful strides. He led her straight into an open elevator, and as the doors closed, the tension between them reached a crescendo. He backed her against the wall and kissed her, bringing those fantasies to life in ways she never could have imagined. And by the time they reached his room—

"Hey, lady! Watch where you're going!"

A hand clamped down on Alyssa's arm and pulled her backward at the same time a car horn blared. She whipped around to find that the hand on her arm belonged to an older man who had just pulled her out of the path of an oncoming car.

She stared at him dumbly, then glanced at the traffic whizzing by. Good Lord. What was the *matter* with her?

She blinked, bringing herself back to reality. "Thank you," she told the man. "I—I don't know what I was thinking."

He gave her a smile. "You must have been day-dreaming."

"Yes," she said. "I guess I was."

"Better be more careful next time," he said as he continued down the street.

Alyssa stood there for a moment, collecting her wits and chastising herself for walking around in traffic like some kind of loony romantic with her head in the clouds. She'd spent a lot of time in the past six months thinking about what had happened in Seattle, but this was the first time that preoccupation had nearly gotten her killed. In every other aspect of her life, she had her head on straight. So why was it that the memory of that man could still make her behave like an idiot?

Oh, hell. She knew why. Because the week she'd spent with him had been the most incredible experience of her life and no man since had measured up. Not one of them had even come close.

Particularly the man she'd met today.

She'd left the restaurant a few minutes ago, thankful she'd agreed to meet him for an early lunch and not dinner. Of course, for the right man, she could have stretched her hour-long lunch into two, but this guy hadn't even been worth a coffee break.

Not that he was unattractive. He was tall and blond with surfer-boy good looks—every woman in the place had noticed him. Unfortunately he'd turned out to be the most smug, self-centered, self-important man she'd ever met.

The light turned red and the Walk sign came on. Alyssa had just stepped off the curb when she heard a voice behind her.

"Alyssa! Wait!"

She turned to see her sister, Kim, hurrying down the sidewalk toward her, moving clumsily in her too-tall heels, the breeze swirling her hair into a copper cloud around her head. She stopped in front of Alyssa, breathing hard.

Alyssa looked at her incredulously. "Kim? What are you doing here?"

"I was sitting in the coffeehouse across the street from the restaurant, waiting for you to come out. But you left so quickly I had a hard time catching up." She wiped a strand of windblown hair from her face and flashed Alyssa a big grin. "So? How was your date with Tom?"

Oh, Lord. That goofy smile again. Ever since Kim had gotten engaged, she'd become The Stepford Sister, with a mission to make Alyssa as ecstatically happy as she was. Unfortunately that meant setting her up with anyone she could find who was male and had a pulse. Since Alyssa had been transferred from Seattle several months ago, Kim had talked her into four blind dates, and every one of them had been a disaster. And this guy—a neighbor of Kim's fiancé— had been the worst one yet.

"How was it?" Alyssa said. "Well, let's see… have you ever listened to somebody talk about himself?"

"Sure."

"For an entire hour?"

Kim's buoyant smile sank into a frown. "Oh, come on. He couldn't have been that bad."

"Do you know what he does for a living?"

"Yeah. He sells luxury cars. Jeff says he makes a lot of money."

"Oh, yeah. He told me he made big bucks last year, but—*hush, hush*—what the IRS doesn't know won't hurt them."

Kim winced. "Well, if he sells cars, he probably drives a nice one, right?"

"Sure he does. It's very expensive and classy and prestigious, you know, and he told me if I'm very, very lucky, he might take me for a ride in it someday. Wouldn't that be fun?"

Kim's expression grew progressively more pained. She shrugged weakly. "Okay. But at least it sounds as if he likes to talk. Beats the silent type."

"Only if we'd had an actual conversation. It was more like pontification. I got to hear about The World According to Tom. Religion, politics, sex, the stock market—I heard it all. I'd be willing to bet he couldn't even tell you my name."

"Come on, Alyssa. There must have been *something* good about him."

"Kim," she said sharply, "the man could barely eat because he was so busy patting himself on the back!"

Kim held up her palm. "Okay. I get the picture. I just thought you two might get along, you know? After all, you went to the same university."

"So did ten thousand other people."

"So you have nothing in common?"

"Yes. We do. We both have opposable thumbs and

walk upright. But I'm looking for a little more compatibility than being part of the same species."

"But opposites attract. Everyone knows that."

"No, they don't. That's a myth perpetuated by people who screwed up and married somebody totally wrong for them and now they're looking for a way to explain the dumb choice they made."

"Okay, so this one didn't work out. But there's still that other guy Jeff works with. The one who—"

Alyssa held up her hand. "No. No more blind dates. Just let me make my own choices from now on, okay?"

"So the men you pick will be better?"

"Yes!"

"Like Mr. Wonderful in Seattle? The man who had an affair with you for a week, lied to you about who he was, then disappeared without a trace?"

Alyssa cringed. Whenever she thought about that time in Seattle, she tried very hard to edit out the way it had ended. The week they'd spent together had been incredible, and not just because of the sex. He said he'd never been to Seattle before, so she'd shown him the sights, taking him to museums and parks and restaurants and enjoying his company more with every moment that had passed. She'd shared more intimate details about her life with him than with any man she'd ever known. She'd told him about her family, her job, her volunteer work, and he'd listened with rapt attention, as if she were the most fascinating woman he'd ever met. She knew she couldn't have been. Not even close. She didn't consider herself to be an unattractive woman, but fascinating she wasn't.

Still, in spite of her rational, reasonable nature that told her how crazy it was, she'd begun to imagine what forever with him might be like. Then she'd awoken one morning to find him gone, with only a cursory note left behind. *It's been fun, but I have to go. Derek.*

She'd told herself to let it drop, to forget him, to pretend the week had never happened, because it clearly hadn't meant as much to him as it had to her. But she couldn't stop herself from trying to find him. And that was when she'd made the most painful discovery of all: every word out of his mouth had been a lie.

Derek Stafford didn't exist. Not in Kansas City, anyway. He'd never worked for Primus Engineering, because it didn't exist, either. He hadn't attended the University of Kansas and Oak Park High School had never heard of him. And slowly she'd realized that while she'd told him everything about herself, he'd offered her almost nothing in return aside from a few basic facts, all of which had turned out to be lies.

She'd felt like a fool. How could she have fallen so hard for a man who hadn't cared about her in the least? Of course, she was acting like an even bigger fool now for wasting time thinking about him at all.

Kim was right. Anything beat a man who was there one day, gone the next, with no goodbye, not even a halfhearted attempt at the old "It's not you, it's me" excuse. Just a note on his pillow and a trail of lies to remember him by.

"He was probably married, you know," Kim said.

"I know."

"Or just a world-class jerk."

"I know."

"Or both."

Alyssa sighed. "I know."

"You need to stay away from guys like him. Go for ones who'll offer you some kind of future."

"Who are also self-important snobs?"

"Okay, then, tell me. If Tom was a dud, what *are* you looking for in a man?"

She didn't know, exactly. It was so hard to describe the man she saw in her head sometimes that it would sound stupid to say it out loud. She wanted a man who was interesting. A man who was exciting, who knew how to excite her.

Her mystery man in Seattle.

He lied to you and left you, and you're still obsessing? What's the matter *with you?*

Kim sighed. "Look. All I'm trying to say is that you may be looking for something that's just not reality. If you're still waiting for that dashing man to ride up on his white horse and sweep you off your feet, you're going to be alone for the rest of your life."

Intellectually, Alyssa knew her sister was right. Still, something inside her said it was better to be alone than with a man who demanded everything and gave nothing.

"After all," Kim went on, "you're pushing thirty. You need to be thinking about settling down."

"I've got a good job. I don't need a man to take care of me."

"You've got a job that requires you to work twelve hours a day and pays you for eight. Lawrence Teague is a gazillionaire, but does he pay you what you're worth? If you didn't get an apartment out of the deal, it'd be slave wages."

"I make enough. And I like my job."

"Right. Running in circles for a bunch of rich people. Sounds like a real blast to me."

Kim just didn't get it. Yes, the people who lived at the Waterford were wealthy. After all, it was arguably the most prestigious apartment building in the city of Dallas, one of seven identical buildings owned by Starlight Properties in major metro areas across the country. It climbed twenty-three stories into the North Dallas skyline, offering housekeeping services, a state-of-the-art security system, an on-site spa and hair salon, as well as a health club. As Tenant Relations Manager, it was a challenging task for Alyssa to keep everyone in the building happy and life running smoothly, but she thrived on it.

"Speaking of Mr. Teague," Alyssa said, "he's flying from Houston to Dallas early tomorrow morning. I'm picking him up at the airport."

"Good. That'd be a great time to ask him for a raise."

Alyssa ignored her sister's remark, thinking instead about her most important task whenever Mr. Teague came to town: making sure he got star treatment. That meant picking him up in a limousine, putting fresh flowers in his suite, having his clothes cleaned and pressed if necessary, making reservations wherever he chose to dine. He might own the building, but she was the hostess there to welcome him to his home away from home.

Alyssa's cell phone rang and she pulled it out and

put it to her ear. As soon as she heard the panicked voice speaking broken English interspersed with Spanish expletives, she knew her problem-solving abilities were about to be put to the test.

After determining the gist of the problem, Alyssa hung up and turned to Kim. "One of the housekeepers accidentally broke a vase in the penthouse apartment."

"Oops. Better hope it's something cheap."

"Up there, nothing's cheap." Alyssa shoved the cell phone back into her purse. "Gotta go."

"I'm sorry your date sucked," Kim said. "I'll try to do better next time."

"Kim? Didn't I tell you there isn't going to be a next time?"

Kim just flashed one of her "that's what you think" smiles. Alyssa wanted to scream with frustration. But instead of fighting it, she merely said goodbye and double-timed it up the street to the Waterford. Right now the problem in Gerald Owens's penthouse was more pressing than her problem with her sister's matchmaking.

Okay. A broken vase. That was only a minor crisis, one she could deal with long before Mr. Teague arrived tomorrow morning. By the time he got here, he'd see nothing but a smoothly operated building and four hundred happy tenants.

As DEREK STONE strode through the parking garage of the Waterford, he felt that familiar rush of adrenaline that pulled every nerve taut and heightened all his senses. Even though the intelligence he'd received about this situation was reliable and the job had been scripted right down to the last footstep, that trace of uncertainty kept his head up and his body on full alert.

He passed one late-model luxury vehicle after another, testimonies to the wealth of the people who lived in this building. If Gerald Owens occupied the penthouse, his business of gathering blackmail information on U.S. government officials had to be pretty lucrative. Maybe even as lucrative as Derek's business, which today just happened to involve retrieving blackmail information before it could cause a government incident.

Derek adjusted his earpiece to make sure the communication was loud and clear between him and the surveillance van parked across the street, and then he pulled his backpack more securely over his shoulder. When he reached the door that led to the private elevator lobby, he glanced over his shoulder and saw no one else in the vicinity.

"I'm at the door," he said softly.

Through his earpiece, Derek heard the soft clacking of Kevin's fingers on his computer keyboard. A moment later the door lock clicked open. Derek entered the lobby and headed for the private elevator that led directly to the penthouse suite.

"I'm in," he said.

Derek listened to a few more seconds of Kevin's keyboard clacking and then the lock clicked behind him.

Perfect.

Derek loved tightly integrated high-tech security systems like this one, because it made his job so much easier. Once they were breached, all it took was a few keystrokes to open doors all over the place. Not that the average hacker could penetrate a sophisticated system like the one at the Waterford, but the men on Derek's team left average in the dust.

"Okay," Derek said. "I'm at the elevator."

"I've bypassed the circuit that reads the key card," Kevin said in his ear. "Just punch in the code. It's sixty-eight, fifty-four. That's six, eight, five, four."

Derek entered the numbers and the elevator doors opened.

"You're a genius, Kevin."

"Uh-huh. Can we talk about that raise now?"

"Don't get cocky."

As the elevator ascended, Kevin said, "The doors will open into the apartment itself. You can head to the safe right away."

Two days ago, Derek's contact in Washington had approached him about Congressman Galloway's problem. In spite of the tight time frame and the possibility of a dozen things going wrong, Derek took the job. His team, as always, had risen to the challenge. They'd begun analyzing the intelligence, planning a breach of the building's security system, and surveilling Gerald Owens.

Fortunately for Owens, Derek's contact in Washington didn't want him arrested or charged. He merely wanted the blackmail material Owens had gathered on Congressman Galloway to be retrieved and destroyed. Owens was only the hired help, anyway. Derek's contact didn't know who had ordered the man to gather the blackmail material, and he didn't care. Making arrests in this case would only bring out into the open what needed to stay firmly under the rug—namely, that Galloway had a fondness for dressing in women's clothing. If Derek didn't retrieve the DVD that showed the congressman's fetish in action, one of two things was going to happen on Monday morning. Either Galloway would vote against the trade bill coming to the House floor, a bill that would greatly restrict the import of certain Chinese goods to America, or Galloway would release the DVD to the press, revealing that Galloway was one of those men who knew Victoria's secret. Once his redneck, gun-toting constituency from east Texas got wind of that, Galloway's chances of reelection were nil.

As the elevator neared the top floor of the building, Derek pulled a ski mask from his pocket and put it on. If something went wrong inside the apartment, the last thing he wanted was for somebody to give his description to the police, which could lead to an artist's rendering of his face being splashed all over the evening news. His team worked independently from contract to contract, sanctioned by the federal government but with no traceable ties to it. Translation: *if something goes wrong, you're on your own.*

Derek mentally reviewed the floor plan of the apartment. A study of the architectural drawings of the building had told him where the safe was and the most direct route to it. He couldn't say for sure that the blackmail material would be there—nothing was one-hundred-percent certain—but the intelligence reports had all pointed to this man, this building and this safe. A pair of Derek's men were tailing Owens right now, ensuring that he stayed on the golf course long enough for Derek to break in. The housekeeping staff maintained a rigid schedule, which meant that the maid had already come and gone, and with Kevin in the van opening doors and keeping watch, this job was going to go off without a hitch.

And, most importantly, his team's perfect record would stay intact.

2

As ALYSSA TOSSED the last piece of broken vase into a trash bag, she reluctantly upgraded the crisis from minor to major. The magnitude of the mess and the size of the empty pedestal beside it told her that the vase had been at least four feet tall. And judging from the quality of the rest of the art in Owens's apartment, it had undoubtedly been worth thousands of dollars.

The moment she'd arrived back at the building, she'd taken the lobby elevator to the penthouse floor to find the housekeeper in tears in the master bedroom. The woman told Alyssa that she usually cleaned the penthouse in the morning, but she'd had a doctor's appointment, which meant she'd been late getting to work. Then, because she was running behind, she'd been in a hurry when she was sweeping the hardwood floor and accidentally bumped the pedestal, sending the vase crashing to the floor.

Alyssa assured the poor woman that of course it had been an accident and of course they had insurance to cover such things, but the housekeeper had been so freaked out that Alyssa had sent her to work on another floor. Then she'd taken off her jacket, tossed it onto the bed and cleaned up the mess herself.

In her mind she was already formulating a plan. She'd phone Owens's decorator for the name of the gallery that had sold him the piece to see if they had a similar one. With luck, she could have it in place before Owens returned from his golf game—a weekly appointment he kept without fail—and discovered the empty pedestal. A similar piece of art couldn't replace the one-of-a-kind vase that had been broken, but at least it would let Owens know that she'd made an effort to rectify the mistake in the most expedient and effective way possible. Since he'd only lived in the building a short time, she was especially motivated to solve the problem to his complete satisfaction.

Then, as she was twist-tying the trash bag, she heard a soft whirring noise. The rear elevator?

She froze. It couldn't be. Mr. Owens wasn't due back for two hours. The man never cut short his golf game. Never.

Sensing that something wasn't right, Alyssa stood motionless, the strangest chill skating across the back of her neck. She peeked out of the bedroom into the living room. A man came into view and her heart jolted hard. It wasn't Gerald Owens.

It was a man in a ski mask.

Suppressing a gasp, Alyssa backed away. A burglar? How had he bypassed the security system?

Her jacket was lying on the bed across the room, her phone in the pocket. All she had to do was dial 9-1-1. She started in that direction, only to hear footsteps and realize he was coming toward the bedroom.

With no time to grab her phone, she shifted her gaze wildly around the room, looking for a place to hide. She hurried to the closet and slipped inside, closing the door silently behind her. The closet light was on. But just as she reached up to turn it off, she heard his footsteps and pulled her hand away from the switch. If he saw the light go off, he'd know someone was in the closet.

With every step he took, her heart rate escalated. She clasped her hands together to stop them from trembling, sure he could hear the slightest move she made.

Then she heard nothing. She felt a shot of relief, only to realize that the absence of footsteps indicated that he'd reached the bedroom rug.

Which meant he was right outside the closet door.

DEREK KNELT on the rug in the master bedroom, flipping the corner back to reveal the floor safe. Again, the state-of-the-art technology offered in this building was working against Owens. With the software Derek had access to, the electronic keypad lock was a whole lot easier to crack than a combination lock.

Derek took off his jacket and stuffed it into his backpack, then pulled out his small laptop computer and flipped it on. Using a wireless connection, in a matter of seconds he set up an interface with the lock at its programming port. He hit a few keys, then sat back to wait as the computer ran the possible combination sequences.

"It's only a five-digit combination," he said to Kevin. "We'll be out of here in no time."

"Good. That means I might be able to go fishing this afternoon after all. I hear they're really biting up at Lake Dallas."

Unlike Kevin, Derek was glad this job had come up at the last minute. If it hadn't, he'd have been at a wedding rehearsal right now, of all things. Talk about dodging a bullet. What would have been the point of him being there, anyway? How tough could it be to stand up with Gus at the front of that church and hand him the ring at the right time?

Derek didn't like weddings. They seemed like a whole lot of time and expense to accomplish something that had the same end result as going to a justice of the peace, assuming a man were crazy enough to get tied down in the first place. Unfortunately once Gus had met Sally, Derek hadn't stood a chance of keeping him. Gus had quit the team a year ago, started a security business and then asked Sally to marry him.

Derek couldn't imagine that kind of life. He thrived on the excitement of crisscrossing the country to solve problems that had to stay under the radar of standard law enforcement. He loved the autonomy he had to get the job done any way he saw fit. He had so many aliases for his undercover operations that sometimes he had a hard time remembering his real name. Because of his profession, he'd never even considered tying himself down to a lengthy relationship, much less a marriage. Likewise, was it really fair to expect a woman to tolerate his here-today-gone-tomorrow lifestyle?

Suddenly the words flashed on the screen: *combination found.*

"I'm in," Derek told Kevin. "How's it looking downstairs?"

"Coast is clear."

Derek returned his laptop to the backpack, punched in the code on the keypad, then opened the safe door. He pulled a penlight from his pocket and flicked it on. A sweep of the interior of the safe revealed a small stack of folders. His intelligence said that Owens had yet to deliver the DVD of Galloway to his client, and when Derek opened the top folder, he saw just how dead-on that information was. In the left-hand pocket of the folder, he found a DVD that was labeled clearly with Galloway's name. Owens was a meticulous record-keeper. Derek smiled to himself. Anally retentive criminals made his job so much easier.

"Got it," he told Kevin.

He was about to close the folder and tack it into his backpack when his attention turned to the right pocket of the folder, which contained photos, lists and other information about the blackmail operation. As Derek flipped through the pages, he came to a stunning realization.

He might have solved one problem, but he'd just found five more.

"Holy crap," he said.

"What?" Kevin said.

"It looks as if Galloway isn't the only congressman Owens is blackmailing."

There were photos of several more congressmen, as well as detailed plans for blackmailing each of them. One other congressman shared Galloway's predisposition toward women's clothing. Two had been caught cheating on their wives. Two more were victims of setups that only made it look as if they'd been cheating. But real or staged, it didn't matter. Either one could send a man's reputation right down the toilet.

"How many are we talking?" Kevin asked.

"Five others besides Galloway."

"Why didn't we know about them?"

"Apparently, Galloway is the only one who came forward and asked for help." Derek flipped through a few more pages and saw a schedule of delivery dates. "Right now it looks as if Galloway was the last guy Owens collected information on, and it's the only DVD he hasn't yet sent to his client."

Derek wasn't sure what to do with the file. If Galloway was the only one being blackmailed, he'd take it, along with every other file in the safe. But now that it was clear that other congressmen were involved, he didn't want Owens to know that somebody had broken in. Owens would alert his client in a heartbeat, which meant they wouldn't stand a chance of locating the rest of the blackmail material that had already been delivered.

"Call Washington," Derek told Kevin. "Get in touch with Sedgewick. Tell him the situation. We need some new marching orders."

Derek waited impatiently as Kevin made the call, anxious to get the hell out of this apartment before something else went wrong. Only two minutes passed before he heard Kevin's voice again, but it felt like a hundred.

"What's the word?" Derek asked.

"We need to grab Owens and get him to Washington for interrogation. They need to find out who his client is so they can have a shot at locating the blackmail material before Monday morning. And bring everything else in the safe, too. They want to know what else this guy is up to."

"Okay," Derek said. "Get on the phone to Wilson and McManus and tell them to pick up Owens and deliver him to the Learjet at Love Field."

"Gotcha."

Derek was confident that that part of the plan would come together. His men were as proficient at kidnapping as they were at surveillance.

"Then call Lambert and tell him I need him to fly the plane," Derek said. "Have him meet us at the airfield ASAP."

"Will do."

"I'm coming down now."

Derek grabbed all the folders from the safe and stuck them into his backpack. After closing the safe, he flipped the rug back into place. Then he stopped short.

Had he just seen a shadow move beneath the closet door?

He froze, barely breathing, his gaze fixed on the shadow. Several seconds passed. It moved again.

Someone was in the closet. And whoever it was had undoubtedly heard every word he'd spoken.

ALYSSA SHIFTED nervously from one foot to the other, thinking that an hour had to have passed while she'd been in this closet. And the longer she stood there, the more she realized something was very strange about this situation. Just the fact that the burglar had gotten past the security system to enter the apartment through the back elevator astonished her. Equally amazing was the speed with which he'd broken into the safe. Pretty soon it became clear to her that his running monologue was actually one side of a conversation he was carrying on electronically with someone who was downstairs keeping watch.

And he was saying the strangest things. Blackmailed congressmen? DVDs? Learjets? What was all that about?

Right now, though, she really didn't care. She just wanted him to grab what he'd come for and leave the building so she could get out of this apartment, call the police, then go somewhere and have a good, stiff drink.

Then all at once, the closet door flew open.

Before she could react with anything but a quick yelp of surprise, the man in the ski mask took two steps into the closet, grabbed her and spun her around. He wrapped his arm around her waist and pulled her against him, her back to his chest. When he pressed the barrel of a gun against the side of her neck, she let out a strangled gasp.

"Not a sound," he said. "Not one."

She fell silent, with only the hiss of her panicked breathing breaking the stillness inside the closet.

"Everything's under control," he murmured. "Just sit tight."

Alyssa knew he wasn't talking to her, but to whomever was on the other end of whatever hands-free communication device he was using. For a long time the man stood motionless, his arm clamped tightly around her. Fear raced through her.

"Tell me your name," he said.

"My name? Why—"

"Tell me."

"Uh, Alyssa. Ballard."

The man's chest expanded with a deep, silent breath. "Damn."

For some reason her name seemed to have made him unhappy. Given that he had a gun pressed to her jugular right now, she really wished it hadn't.

"Do you work in this building?" he asked.

"Yes."

Even as Alyssa's heart pounded with apprehension, a sense of sudden recognition came over her. That voice. She'd heard it before. Despite the fact that his words were threatening, the deep, melodic tone of his voice still came through.

But it couldn't be. She was imagining it.

He shifted his hand against her rib cage. She looked down at it and she couldn't believe what she saw. A ring. Sterling silver. Alpha and omega symbols intertwined.

She glanced at his arm wrapped around her, his bicep bulging beneath his black T-shirt, and saw a long, irregular scar that extended the length of his forearm, faded to white but still distinct. The ring she was just now remembering, but his body she'd never forgotten. She'd memorized every inch of it, up to and including that scar.

For a moment she was too stunned to speak. Every second seemed sluggish and protracted as the reality of who he was slowly bared itself. She swallowed hard, trying to find her voice.

"Derek?"

His body stiffened, an involuntary reaction that told her just how right she was. Good Lord. She didn't know how, she didn't know why, but…

It was Derek. He was here. In this building, two thousand miles from the last place she'd seen him. And he was robbing this apartment.

"It's you," she said. "I know it is. Your voice. Your ring. The scar on your arm."

He was silent.

"So this is why you left me in Seattle?" she said, her voice escalating. "Because you're a burglar?"

He said nothing. She squirmed in his arms. "Let me *go!*"

When he continued to hold her tightly, suddenly all the pain and frustration he'd caused her, both here and in Seattle, welled up inside her in a hot mass of anger. The man she'd been so crazy about, the man who'd intrigued her to no end, the man with whom she'd spent one wonderful week and had imagined a thousand more to come…

He was a criminal. And he wasn't going to get away with this.

She lifted her knee, then slammed her heel down hard on his instep. He grunted in pain, loosening his grip on her just enough that she wrenched herself from his arms and shoved him aside to head out of the closet. But before she cleared the doorway, he snaked his arm around her and yanked her back. Only this time he didn't stop there. He pulled a tie off a nearby rack and bound her hands behind her.

"What are you doing?" she shouted, yanking hard

against the tie, unable to believe he'd done it. Unable to believe how *fast* he'd done it.

Ignoring her, he grabbed another tie and gagged her with it, then led her out of the closet and over to the bed, where he sat her down, bound her ankles and tethered her to the bedpost. She fought him every step of the way, but he was bigger than she was and infinitely stronger, and within a few minutes, he had her completely subdued.

He walked away and stood near the wall, his back to her, his shoulders heaving with a few deep breaths. She could almost feel the tension radiating from him. Was it from anger? Indecision? She couldn't tell. When he turned back around, though, he seemed to sigh with resignation.

Then he reached up and pulled off the ski mask.

Alyssa had already known beyond all doubt that it was Derek, but seeing him again like this made emotions swirl wildly inside her. Fear. Surprise. Anger. All of those made sense. But mingling with them was something that made no sense at all—an unwanted rush of the elemental desire she'd felt the first time she'd laid eyes on him. But he was a burglar and a kidnapper. How could she have any feelings of attraction toward him at all?

He came back to the bed and sat beside her, tossing the mask aside. To her surprise, he also disconnected the tiny microphone clipped to his collar. He regarded her silently for a moment, then lifted his hand to brush a wayward strand of her hair gently back over her shoulder. His fingertips grazed her neck, sending shivers all the way down her spine.

No. He had no right to touch her. None at all. She turned away sharply, glaring at him out of the corner of her eye.

"Alyssa," he said, "listen to me. I'm in a tight spot here. No matter what this looks like, I'm not a burglar. Not the kind you think I am, anyway. And as far as tying you up like this, I have no choice. I can't risk you telling anyone what you just overheard. I'll explain everything to you later, including what happened in Seattle, but I have to take care of a few things first."

He lifted his hand and rested his palm along the side of her neck, trailing his thumb in soft strokes just beneath her jaw. In spite of the situation, her mind flashed back to those scorching nights they'd spent together in a tangle of bedsheets, making love far into the night. Just the memory made her want to believe everything he was telling her.

No. She had to stay focused. No matter what he said, he was a burglar, and a hell of a good liar. God only knew what he really intended to do with her.

When she jerked her face away from him again, he let out a soft sigh, trailing his hand down her arm before finally pulling it away altogether.

"You'll be here alone," Derek told her. "Owens won't be coming back."

When her eyes widened, he shook his head. "Take it easy, Alyssa. We don't kill people. Owens is just being…diverted."

Diverted? What did that mean? And who the hell was "we"?

Derek rose from the bed and disconnected the

phone cord from the wall. He picked up his gun from where he'd tossed it on the bed and stuck it into his jeans, then took a lightweight jacket from his back-pack and put it on, pulling it down over the weapon. He grabbed the ski mask and stuffed it into the pocket of the jacket. Slinging the backpack over his shoulder, he turned to Alyssa one last time.

"I should be back within the hour."

He left the room. Alyssa heard his footsteps as he walked to the elevator and the faint sound of the doors opening and closing.

And then he was gone.

3

DEREK STEPPED OFF the elevator and walked through the parking garage, moving quickly and decisively even as his mind was spinning in a dozen different directions.

When he'd grabbed Alyssa in that closet, for a few seconds he hadn't been able to move. To think. To believe who he had his arms around. But there was no mistaking that mass of blond hair, those green eyes and that slight, willowy figure he remembered as clearly as if he'd seen her yesterday. He'd known she worked in a building that was identical to this one in Seattle, but he'd never imagined that he'd find her here. He'd asked her what her name was just to ensure that the concept most people believed in—that everybody has a double somewhere—hadn't come into play.

It hadn't. It was Alyssa.

And then she'd said his name. Softly. Tentatively. Even after six months, she'd still recognized tiny details she never should have remembered. His ring. His scar.

His voice, for God's sake.

He'd hated like hell having to manhandle her the

way he had, not to mention having to tie her up and leave her there. But he had to make sure Owens got to the airport ASAP, and she clearly hadn't been in the mood to listen to anything he'd had to say. Until he had the chance to calm her down and find out just how inclined she was to tell the world what she'd overheard, restraining her had been his only option.

He exited the parking garage and walked to the van waiting on the street outside the building. After climbing into the driver's seat, he tossed his backpack down and shut the door.

Kevin emerged from the back of the van and flopped into the passenger seat. "What the hell was going on up there? I lost communication with you for a few minutes."

"Somebody was in the apartment. She heard everything."

"She said your name. She knows who you are."

"Yes. She's…" The last thing Derek wanted was to delve into his history with Alyssa. "She's an acquaintance."

"Oh, boy. So where is she now?"

"Tied up in the bedroom."

Kevin stared at him, dumbfounded. "What?"

"I left her tied up in the bedroom."

"So what are you going to do with her?"

Derek paused. "To tell you the truth, I'm not sure. Once we get Owens on the plane, I'll come back and deal with her. By that time I'll have something figured out."

"And if you let her go and she talks?"

"I'll make sure she doesn't."

"But how—"

"I said I'd handle it."

Kevin looked at him skeptically, but he'd never been one to overstep his bounds. Finally he simply nodded.

"Did you get in touch with the team?" Derek asked.

"Wilson and McManus say they'll have no trouble grabbing Owens. But there's a problem with Lambert."

"A problem?"

"He's got the flu. Woke up with it this morning. A hundred and three fever. Can't stop puking. Says he couldn't possibly get a plane off the ground."

Derek just stared at Kevin, unable to believe that not a damned thing was going right with this job. First, the blackmailing problem he'd set out to solve was far bigger than he'd realized. Then he'd had to take a woman hostage to keep her from talking—a woman he never would have considered tying up in bed unless she'd smiled pretty, got naked and asked him to. And now he had a pilot who couldn't stop hugging the toilet long enough to fly to Washington.

Derek hated this. *Hated* it. His team's reputation was built on jobs going off cleanly without a hitch, and now he was on the verge of having to phone Washington and admit he couldn't pull this one off because he had no pilot.

No. He wasn't going to do that. Failure was *not* an option.

Derek started the van.

"Where are you going?" Kevin asked.

"St. Andrews."

"The church?"

"Yes."

"Wait a minute. Isn't that where Gus is getting married tomorrow?"

"Yes."

Derek wheeled the van away from the curb and hit the gas.

"You're gonna get him to fly the plane?" Kevin asked.

"That's right."

"But he quit the team a year ago."

"Do you know any other pilot we can get on short notice who can fly a Learjet to Washington *and* who won't wonder why he's transporting a guy in handcuffs and handing him off to federal agents?"

Kevin sighed. "Good point."

Ten minutes later Derek pulled up in front of St. Andrews. He turned to Kevin. "Get in the back. I don't want Gus to see you and think we're double-teaming him."

"And if he won't come?"

"That's when we can double-team him."

Derek parked behind a black stretch SUV. Nearby, several men milled around whom he took to be the other groomsmen. A white limousine was parked in front of the black one. Clustered around it was a group of young women who appeared to be the bridesmaids.

Derek checked his watch. It looked as if the rehearsal was over and the men were heading out to the golf course before the rehearsal dinner tonight.

As soon as Derek stepped out of the van, Gus spotted him and walked over.

"About time you showed up," he said with a smile, clapping Derek on the shoulder. Then he lowered his voice. "Tell me the truth. You asked for that job just to get out of the rehearsal, didn't you?"

Derek was relieved to see Gus in a better mood now than he had been when Derek had phoned earlier to tell him he had to miss the rehearsal. Of course, as soon as Gus found out why he was here now, that smile would be history.

"Sorry, man," Derek said. "Duty called."

"That's the story of your life."

"Used to be the story of yours, too."

"Not anymore." Gus leaned in and spoke quietly. "Guess I should have expected something like this when I asked you to be my best man, huh? 'Sorry, buddy. Can't make the rehearsal. Gotta tend to a congressman with his pants down.' Or his panties down, as the case may be." He gave Derek a smile, his voice still low and confidential. "So how'd it go this morning?"

"Not well," he said quietly. "That's why I need a favor."

Gus's grin evaporated. "What favor?"

"I need you to fly the Learjet to Washington."

Gus just stared at him. "Come again?"

"Learjet. Washington. ASAP. I'm in a bind, and I need you."

Gus held up his palms. "No way. I'm out of that business."

He turned and walked away. Derek followed, finally grabbing his arm, but he shook it off.

"It'll take a few hours, max," Derek said.

"I'm getting *married*."

"Not until tomorrow."

"So why aren't you sending Lambert?"

Derek sighed. "He has the flu."

Gus looked flabbergasted. "The flu? The *flu?*" He glanced over his shoulder, then dropped his voice to an irate whisper. "I once flew a C-5 Galaxy over enemy territory when I had malaria, for God's sake. Tell him to get his ass out of bed and fly the freakin' plane!"

"I was with you when you flew that plane. My life flashed before my eyes."

"This is my *wedding* we're talking about. Find yourself another pilot."

Derek glanced over to see a few of the groomsmen staring at them. He lowered his voice. "Look, I know it's a hell of a lot to ask. But there's a guy I have to get to D.C. for interrogation, and I have to do it right now. I took this job, and it's my responsibility to see it through."

"Right. Your responsibility. Not mine."

"Gus—"

"No! There's a reason I'm out of the business. So I can have a life that doesn't involve having to do this short-fuse crap anymore."

"Fly to D.C., hit the tarmac, unload the cargo, do a one-eighty and head back. That's all I need." Derek could see his friend starting to waver. "Come on, Gus. Haven't we always watched each other's backs? Always?"

Gus blew out a breath. "Playing the loyalty card is really low."

"Hey, I'm stuffing myself into a tuxedo for you tomorrow. The least you can do is fly to Washington for me today."

Gus closed his eyes and shook his head.

"It's really no big deal," Derek went on. "You'll be back in time for the rehearsal dinner tonight. Hell, all we were going to do this afternoon is play golf anyway."

"I like golf."

"You also like to fly. Get in the van, and I'll fill you in on the way to Love Field."

"I need to talk to Sally first."

"No. If you talk to her now, you'll never get out of here. Phone her from the airfield. Tell her something came up, but you'll be at the rehearsal dinner tonight."

Derek opened up the passenger door. Gus stared at the van, then back at Derek. "You owe me for this."

"You bet. Just name your price. *After* you get the guy to Washington."

Gus hauled himself into the van. Derek stepped into the driver's seat, started the engine and hit the gas. He wanted to get out of there before Gus saw his bride and changed his mind.

"Unbelievable," Kevin said from the back of the van. "He talked you into it."

Gus gave Kevin a deadpan look. "I'm a sucker for a sob story." He turned back to Derek. "So, fill me in. Who's my cargo?"

Derek gave him the short version of the predicament they were in, judiciously leaving out the part about Alyssa. No need to go there, particularly when it was a loose end he planned to tie up on his own later.

"So we've got to get this guy to Washington for interrogation," he told Gus, "or come Monday morning, either the president's trade bill is going down because a few congressmen don't want to see themselves in compromising positions all over cable news, or cable news is going to have a field day when they get hold of—" He stopped short, looking in the rearview mirror. "Damn it."

"What?"

"Somebody's following us."

Gus glanced in the side mirror. "That blue Mustang?"

"Yeah. He's been hugging my bumper for the past few miles. This makes the fourth time I've changed lanes and he has, too."

"It's Barry Sutton," Gus said. "Hard to miss that car. I saw him getting into it as we were leaving."

Derek came to a red light and braked to a halt. "Any idea why he's after us?"

"He's a reporter who used to cover big stories but got busted to the society section. Maybe he's looking for news from my wedding that's a little more interesting than what color the mother of the bride is wearing."

"Then we'd better lose him." Derek put two hands on the wheel. "Hang on."

Derek hit the gas and wheeled hard to the left,

hopped the curb to the median and made a U-turn against the red light. He gunned it for fifty yards, then turned into a strip-center parking lot and headed down the service alley. Checking his rearview mirror, he saw Sutton's Mustang still sitting at the red light.

"He's not following," Derek said.

"Hell, no, he's not," Gus muttered, rubbing his neck. "Did you have to jump the damned curb?"

Derek grinned. "You've gotten soft, Gus. That's tragic."

"No. Tragic is having to miss my golf game this afternoon."

"Golf. Now, there's some excitement."

"It's all the excitement I'm looking for these days."

"Come on. Think about all the fun we used to have. You loved every minute of it."

"Yeah. I did. But I love Sally more."

He spoke with such conviction that Derek knew there was more to his relationship with his fiancée than some hot sex with a pretty lady. Gus had quit the team and started his own business for one reason only: so he could have that one special woman to come home to for the rest of his life.

When Derek thought about that, for some reason Alyssa's face flashed through his mind.

No. Stop thinking about her like that.

He told himself, as he had for the past six months, that thoughts like those would eventually get him into trouble. Soon he'd be roped and tied like Gus, playing house with his wife and golfing with his buddies. But he just wasn't cut out for that kind of life, and he had yet to meet a woman who could convince him that he was.

FORTUNATELY THE REST of the job went off like clockwork, which was a big relief for Derek after everything that had gone wrong. Wilson and McManus had Owens waiting at Love Field when they arrived. In fewer than three hours, the blackmailer would be in Washington. With any luck, Owens would crack and give the interrogators the name of his client and the location of the blackmail material. Then they'd call Derek in one more time to retrieve it, and this problem would be put to bed once and for all.

But right now he had to deal with Alyssa.

Kevin stayed in the van across the street from the Waterford, punching his computer to let Derek back into the building. As Derek ascended the elevator to the penthouse, his heart was pounding a little harder than usual. He'd rather take a beating than face Alyssa after what had happened in there.

As the elevator doors opened, he spoke into the microphone, telling Kevin he'd be out of touch for a short time and to stay put until he contacted him again. Then he flipped the microphone off and made his way to the master bedroom.

Alyssa sat on the bed exactly where he'd left her, but the anger she'd displayed earlier seemed to have disappeared. Instead, when she looked up at him, her green eyes were full of the pain of betrayal. And he was the reason why.

Stop beating yourself up. You had no choice.

When he settled beside her on the bed, she shrank away from him. He sighed heavily.

"I'm going to untie you," he told her, "but I can't let you leave yet. We need to talk. Agreed?"

She nodded.

He removed the gag first, easing it away carefully, wincing when he saw the red, irritated skin at the corners of her mouth. She stretched her jaw stiffly, refusing to look at him. When he untied her ankles, then her hands, he was dismayed to see the ties had left their mark there, too.

"I can't believe you did this," she said, rubbing her wrists. "I can't believe—"

He touched his hand to her arm. When she jerked it away from him and stood, he wondered if she intended to bolt from the room. Instead she merely walked several paces away and stopped, her back to him, rubbing her upper arms with her palms.

"You left me in Seattle," she said, her voice quivering as if she were on the verge of tears. "After a whole week together, suddenly you were gone. And now…and now *this*."

"Alyssa—"

"How could you *do* this to me?"

With that, she dropped her head to her hands and began to cry.

Derek felt a shot of apprehension. He'd sailed through military combat with flying colors. He ran a team of stealth operatives, keeping his cool in situations unimaginable to the average man. His pain tolerance was legendary. He had very few weaknesses.

But watching a woman cry was one of them.

He'd expected her to be fighting mad. That he could have dealt with just fine. But now that she was falling apart, he had no clue what to do.

"Alyssa…"

He rose from the bed and went to her, putting his hand on her shoulder. To his surprise, she turned quickly, ducked her head and fell against him. He automatically wrapped his arms around her and she laid her head against his chest, her body shaking with sobs.

"You're a liar," she said, crying so hard she could barely speak.

"I know, but—"

"And a thief."

"Well, technically I am, but—"

"And a bully."

A bully? Now, wait a minute. He'd been called a lot of things in his life, but never that. He liked to think he wasn't one of those guys who acted tough just for the sake of intimidating people, but clearly she thought he was.

But even as she berated him with one accusation after another, she clutched her arms more tightly around him, as if she was begging him to tell her that none of her words were true.

Unfortunately most of them were.

"Alyssa, sweetheart, listen to me. I had no choice. I had to—"

All at once she slid out of his arms and pushed him away, so hard that he stumbled backward. It startled him so much that a second passed before he realized what else she'd done.

She'd grabbed the gun from the small of his back.

He started toward her, but she'd already raised the weapon. Stopping short, he held his palms in the air, unable to believe that the woman he'd thought was crying had a face as dry as dust.

"You're right, Derek," Alyssa said. "We have some talking to do."

4

ALYSSA WASN'T too thrilled to be holding a gun on anyone, particularly this man, because even with a firearm she wasn't completely sure she was the one in control. But she wasn't about to let him see her apprehension. And after all, it was a dream scenario, wasn't it? Getting the opportunity to hold a gun on him and demand answers to the questions that had been driving her crazy for the past six months?

"I thought you were crying," Derek said.

She made a scoffing noise. "Over you? A man who used me, lied to me, then left me? Hardly."

She hoped to see him at least wince at that, but his expression held steady. The only indication of any emotion was a narrowing of his eyes as he assessed the situation. The gun felt heavy in her hands and she shifted it a little to get a better grip.

He held up his palms. "Be careful with that gun, sweetheart. The trigger's pretty touchy."

"Stop patronizing me."

"Ever fire a gun before?"

"No, but it can't be all that hard. All I have to do is pull the trigger."

He eyed her carefully. "You and I both know you won't shoot me."

"Maybe not. But I might take out that picture window over there. I'll bet a little glass raining down twenty-three stories would draw a crowd."

He flicked his gaze to the window, his brows pulling together as he seemed to consider the consequences of that. Slowly he looked back. "Okay, then. What do you want?"

"First of all, let's see some ID."

"It wouldn't tell you a thing."

"It would tell me your real name."

"It would tell you what my name is today."

"Which is not Derek."

"Yes, it is. That part is the truth."

"But the last name you told me was a lie."

"So you tried to look me up?"

Suddenly she felt silly about that. Chasing after a man who clearly hadn't cared about her in the least? What would she have done if she'd found him?

"Call it curiosity," she said. "And I found out everything you told me was a lie."

When Derek gave her nothing in return but cold silence, Alyssa felt a shot of irritation. "Never mind. I don't care about all that. Just tell me why you broke into this apartment."

He paused for a moment, as if deciding just how much to reveal. "I work for the government."

"Since when do they employ burglars?"

"That's not what I am."

"You sure look like one to me."

"I retrieve things that can't be recovered in conventional ways."

"Such as blackmail material on half a dozen U.S. congressmen?"

His gaze held steady. "So you heard."

"I heard. And Gerald Owens is doing the blackmailing?"

He paused. "Yes."

"Why does he want to blackmail congressmen?"

"I can't tell you that."

"What's on the DVDs you're after?"

"I can't tell you that, either."

"Tell me about the Learjet hangared at Love Field."

He was silent.

"Oh, I get it. You could tell me, but then you'd have to kill me?"

His jaw tightened with irritation. "You don't have any idea what you've stepped into here. It's not a good thing that you overheard what you did."

"Oh, really?"

"Yes. Whenever there's a breach of security, standard operating procedure is for me to report it to my superiors. But if I'd done that, you'd be in the company of federal agents right now, being persuaded that it's in your best interest not to tell a soul what you know."

"That's kind of B-movie, isn't it?" But a tremor of uneasiness crept up her spine.

"Even the most outlandish fiction has some basis in fact."

"But if you really are the good guys—"

"The good guys sometimes do wrong things for the right reasons."

"So if you're one of those good guys, what stopped you? Why didn't you just turn me in?"

He took a casual step toward her, but there was nothing casual about the expression on his face. It had shifted into the one he'd worn that first night she'd seen him in the hotel bar, full of the kind of sexual promise that had captured her attention at a single glance.

"Because," he said, "I wanted to be the one doing the persuading."

Involuntary shivers of excitement raced through her, filling her mind with images of their sweat-sheened bodies as they'd made love for hours on end…

Wait a minute. What was she thinking?

She jerked her mind out of the past and back to the present. *Fool me once, shame on you. Fool me twice…*

She stood straighter, tightening her fist on the grip of the gun. "Derek?"

"Yes?"

"You can take your sexual manipulation and shove it."

He bowed his head with frustration, then looked back up. "Alyssa—"

"I have control of this situation, and you don't like that. So you don't mind manipulating me however you think you need to so I won't talk. You seduced me in Seattle, then lied to me, and you're not above doing it again."

"I haven't lied to you. I told you why I'm here."

"You've admitted only what you know I overheard."

He was silent.

Alyssa's anger escalated. "I want the whole story. I want to know why you left me before and exactly what you're doing here now, or I swear to God I'll blast a hole right through that window."

Derek said nothing.

"Damn it, after what you did to me, you *owe* me the truth!"

"I can't tell you the truth!"

"Fine. Then I'll just let the authorities deal with you." She swung the gun around and pointed it at the window.

"Alyssa, don't!"

Derek dove at her, wrapping his arms around her waist. The moment their bodies collided, she inadvertently tightened her finger on the trigger.

A shot exploded.

As Derek's momentum knocked them both to the ground, whatever glass wasn't on its way to the pavement twenty-three stories below clattered to the bedroom floor. Alyssa lay beneath Derek, feeling totally disoriented and flabbergasted beyond words, because she hadn't actually intended to pull the trigger. She'd just been so angry, and threatening him had felt so incredibly satisfying.

Derek yanked the gun from her hand and stuffed it into the back of his jeans. Slapping his palms on the floor, he levered himself to his feet, then hauled her up beside him. He pulled her over to the bed, grabbed his backpack and her jacket, and dragged her out of the bedroom.

"Derek!" she said. "What are you doing?"

"Security's going to be up here any minute. And the cops won't be far behind."

"No! I'm not going anywhere with you!"

He continued to pull her along, though, giving her no choice. She saw the elevator ahead and he hauled her inside, then hit the button. The doors closed and the elevator descended.

Alyssa felt a glimmer of fear. After all, she didn't know this man. He'd danced around his true identity the entire week they'd spent together in Seattle, so she'd never known who he really was. Even if he was telling her the truth now, that he worked for the government...

Sometimes they do the wrong things for the right reasons.

Maybe he did, too.

They reached the first floor and the doors opened. The lobby was empty. Derek strode out of the elevator and tried to open the door leading to the parking garage.

It was locked.

He rattled the door, then turned back. "What's going on?"

For a moment Alyssa wasn't sure. Then she remembered. "Security has probably overridden the main system with the emergency circuit that locks down the building. Nobody can get in or out."

"Will the guards come to check out the back elevator?"

"If they don't, they're not doing their jobs."

Derek spit out a curse. Alyssa couldn't help feeling a glimmer of satisfaction. "Looks like you've got a problem, doesn't it?"

He spun around. "Damn it, Alyssa! Don't you get this?" He strode back to her. "My team operates under the radar. If I'm caught, nobody in Washington is going to admit I exist. That means that if I'm arrested, they won't do a thing to help me. I swear to God, I'm one of the good guys, but if you blow the whistle on me when the security guards show up, I'll likely be convicted and do jail time. Now, is that what you really want?"

Alyssa swallowed hard. Could he be telling her the truth?

The pieces fit. Everything she'd overheard pointed to him being exactly who he said he was—a government operative with orders to retrieve blackmail information on congressmen. If all that was true, if he really was one of the good guys, then if she turned him in...

"Alyssa?" he said. "Can you get me out of here?"

The soft plea she heard in his voice gave her the feeling that his life really was in her hands. She pictured him in a jail cell, lost to the world for years, all because he'd followed government orders. Her resolve began to disintegrate.

Trust him.

Even though there was no logical reason for her to act on those words, they sounded inside her head until they screamed so loudly she couldn't ignore them.

She let out a breath of resignation. "Yes. I can get you out of here."

"How?"

"My key card will override the lockdown mechanism. It's in the pocket of my jacket."

He pulled out the card, tossed her jacket to her, then turned to look at the door. "There's no reader on the inside."

"It's embedded between the door and the door frame about a foot up from the lock."

Derek pulled out her key card and swiped it in the place she'd indicated. The door clicked and he started to open it.

Alyssa grabbed his arm. "What if you're seen leaving when the building's locked down? Won't that be suspicious?"

"I don't have any choice."

Trust that he's telling you the truth. He needs your help.

"My apartment is on the third floor. I can take you there. There's a stairwell right outside this door."

"Let's go."

Derek opened the door and they slipped into the parking garage, then hurried to the stairwell. Moments later they emerged into the third-floor hallway. It was vacant. They rushed four doors down to Alyssa's apartment and Derek used her key card to open the door. Once they'd slipped inside, he closed the door and flipped the lock.

Alyssa walked to the window. Two police cars had pulled up in front of the building. "The police are here. They'll investigate."

"That's okay," Derek said. "They can't know for sure it was a gun that made that noise. They won't even be able to tell that a bullet went through the window unless they perform forensic tests on the glass fragments. With no other signs of foul play, it's doubtful they'd do that."

"And if they do?"

"They'll discover that a bullet shattered the glass. But they still won't have a clue where it came from."

She turned around to see Derek flick a switch on the microphone clipped to his shirt and speak into it. "Everything's under control," he said quietly. "Stay put and I'll get back to you soon."

After flicking it off again, he removed the mike from his shirt and stuffed it into the pocket of his jacket. He set her key card on the table beside the door, then fixed his dark eyes on her in a narrow gaze.

After the flurry of activity, her apartment felt still and quiet, with a sense of anticipation hovering in the air. She remembered the twinge of panic she'd felt that first night when she'd wondered if she'd taken too big a risk by going behind closed doors with a man like him.

She felt exactly the same way now.

"You did the right thing," Derek said quietly. "I know you're not sure about that, but you did."

"You're right. I'm not sure about anything where you're concerned."

She meant for her words to sound sharp and definitive, accusatory, even, because she had no intention of ever letting him know how much he'd hurt her. Instead there was a melancholy tone to her voice and, by the way his expression shifted, she could tell he'd picked up on it instantly.

He shrugged the backpack off his shoulder, let it slide down his arm, then caught it and lowered it to the floor. After a moment he walked toward her, his boots clicking softly on her oak floor, coming to a halt a few feet away.

"You're the last person I expected to find here," he told her.

"I worked at an identical building in Seattle."

"I know. But this is Dallas."

"I was transferred. My family is here."

He nodded. For a long time he stared at her silently, and she didn't have a clue what he was thinking.

"Alyssa," he said, "about what happened in the penthouse—"

"You don't have to tell me to keep quiet about this. I won't say anything."

"I know you won't."

"Then what?"

"I don't know. The second I saw you again...realized it was you..."

He moved closer as he talked, an aura of sexual energy surrounding him, an almost tangible thing that seemed to inhale and exhale with a life of its own. His gaze played over her face as if he was seeing it for the first time.

"After Seattle," he said, "when you tried to look me up, it was more than curiosity, wasn't it?"

Yes, it was more than curiosity. It was a driving need to know what had happened to the man she'd fallen for so completely and who had left without a trace.

"Don't flatter yourself," she said. She turned away to toss her jacket on the sofa, only to have him ease up behind her. The moment she felt the heat of his body bridging the scant space between them, she froze. He settled his hands on her upper arms. She shook him off and spun around.

"Don't touch me."

"You didn't turn me in."

"I still can."

"You won't."

"Just because I don't want to see you in jail doesn't mean I want anything else from you. And the only reason we spent that week together in Seattle was because of who I *thought* you were: a security specialist for a manufacturing company in Kansas City." She paused. "A man who would never think of walking away without a word."

"Maybe so. But we spent that first night together because we couldn't keep our hands off each other."

God, he was so right about that. The memory of those few hours could still distract her into walking right off curbs into oncoming traffic.

"Don't you remember?" he murmured, edging close to her again. "Don't you remember what it felt like to be together?"

Suddenly the memories weren't just shadowy images anymore, faded with time. The look in his eyes and his soft words brought them to life again until they were bright and sharp and enticing, mingling with the reality of this moment. He was back, making her feel those things all over again, and she just couldn't resist him. If she had one fatal flaw, succumbing to this man was it. She bowed her head in a weak protest.

"Derek," she said, "don't you know what you do to me?"

"What?" he whispered. "Tell me."

Now he stood so near that she swore she could feel

the rise and fall of his chest with every breath he took, so near she had to tilt her head back to meet his eyes. Even if she'd known what to say, her throat was too tight to release the words. Blood rushed to her head and throbbed in her ears, making her so dizzy she couldn't think straight.

Still staring at her intently, Derek laid a hand on her upper arm, then slid it down to encircle her wrist, pressing his thumb to her pulse point. "Never mind," he murmured. "I can feel it."

He was right. Her heart was racing like mad. He pulled up her hand and held it against his chest.

"Feel that," he whispered. "You do the same thing to me."

Just her palm pressed against the hard muscles of his chest put her in danger of hyperventilating. From the first moment Derek had caught her eye at that hotel bar, she'd had the feeling he could read her every thought. And if he was doing it right now, he knew just how much she wanted him no matter how wrong it was.

"I'm such a fool," she said.

"Why?"

"I believed everything you told me before, and here I am believing you all over again."

"I haven't lied to you. Not this time."

"No lies, maybe. Just a few gaping omissions."

"You can believe this," he said, slipping his arm around her waist. "Not a day has gone by in the last six months that I haven't thought about seeing you again. Not one."

With that, he dragged her to him and kissed her.

5

THERE WAS NOTHING subtle about Derek's kiss, nothing tentative. It was the wild, careless, demanding statement of a man who knew what he wanted, had wanted it for a very long time, and now that he had the opportunity, he was taking it.

Memories came flooding back to Alyssa. Their first night together. The elevator doors had barely closed before his mouth had been on hers, kissing her exactly as he was now, before he took her to his room and made love to her for hours. She'd almost exploded with that feeling of love at first sight, something she'd never believed in before but that had suddenly been happening to her. And she'd had the unmistakable feeling that fate had put her in that bar that night so she could meet the man of her dreams.

Now his hands roamed over her, talented hands that had always known exactly where to caress her to make her crazy with desire. She clung to his shoulders, then circled her arms around his neck, wanting more, meeting him kiss for kiss, touch for touch, unable to get enough of him.

"I can't believe you're here," she said on a gasping breath. "It's been such a long time..."

"I know, sweetheart, I know."

"You left me. Why did you leave me?"

"I must have been out of my mind."

The words tumbled out of her mouth of their own accord, ill-advised words to go with her ill-advised actions, but she couldn't have stopped either of them if she'd tried. The moment he kissed her, her defenses seemed to melt away and all she knew was that she wanted to feel the excitement all over again.

Then he was pulling her down the hall. This apartment had the same floor plan as her apartment in Seattle, and he probably could have found his way to her bedroom with his eyes closed. He stopped at one point to press her up against the wall and kiss her again—her lips, her throat, the curve of her shoulder—his mouth moving over her in the most shockingly sensual way.

He fumbled with the buttons on her blouse and she thought she'd die from the anticipation she felt. But his hands were too large and his fingers trembling too much to navigate the tiny buttons. Finally he just yanked her shirt from the waistband of her skirt and shoved it up, unhooked her bra, swept the cups aside and ran his hands over her rounded flesh with a groan of satisfaction. He palmed her breasts, lifted them, and then his mouth was on her, hot and moist, every movement of his lips and tongue sending hot tremors right down between her legs. It was good, so good, *too* good, and when she writhed beneath him, he trapped her wrists against the wall and continued his exquisite torture until she thought she'd go out of her mind.

Finally they reached her bedroom. Derek ripped off his jacket and yanked the gun out of the back of his jeans. He slapped the weapon down on her dresser, curled his hand around the back of her neck and pulled her in for another kiss. When she tugged his shirt out of the waistband of his jeans, he tore his mouth away from hers and snatched it over his head. After slinging it aside, he took her by the hand, led her to the bed and ripped the covers back. When he fell onto it, he dragged her down with him, flipping her over and treating her to a series of deep, drugging kisses at the same time that he moved his hand beneath her skirt to stroke her thighs.

This was it. This was what she'd dreamed about in the dark of night for the past six months, and she could hardly breathe for the wild beating of her heart and the knowledge that she was back in his arms again. If only they could stay here forever, right in this place, making love from now until—

Phone. Her phone was ringing.

Alyssa pulled away from Derek and glanced over at it.

"Ignore it," he said.

Gladly, she thought as he pulled her back. After six rings, it fell silent. But when it rang again a few minutes later, Alyssa fumbled her hand to the nightstand, grabbed it and glanced at the Caller ID.

"It's the head of security," she said breathlessly.

"Don't take it."

"I have to. He probably wants to tell me about what happened in the penthouse. It's going to seem strange if he can't find me."

Alyssa sat up, took a deep, calming breath, then hit the talk button. The man reported that there had been an incident in the penthouse and the police were on their way. He went on to say that he figured she'd want to be fully informed so she could smooth this over with Owens when he returned. She told him to give her five minutes, then hung up.

"I have to go," she told Derek.

"Can't the manager handle it?"

"He's away for a few days. I have to take care of this."

With a sigh of resignation, Derek leaned back against the headboard. They stared at each other for a moment, and with the spell broken, suddenly the situation felt awkward. Now that she was starting to get her wits about her, she realized that he'd offered her next to nothing in the way of explanation for his behavior six months ago, yet all he'd had to do was crook his finger and she had succumbed to him all over again.

What in the world had she done?

She turned away and rose from the bed. After hooking her bra, she pulled her blouse down again and tucked it into her skirt. Even when her back was turned, she knew his eyes were on her. They'd spent most of that week in Seattle wearing not a stitch of clothing, but now she felt self-conscious.

She glanced into her dresser mirror to smooth her hair, hoping the flush of her cheeks would fade by the time she made it up to the penthouse. She took a deep breath to steady herself, then walked to her bedroom door. At the last moment she turned back to see Derek still propped against the headboard, his arms crossed over his bare chest, staring at her. Their gazes caught and held for a long, wavering moment, her mind still hot and hazy from their encounter.

Thank God they'd been interrupted, because she needed to ask more questions. Get more answers. When she got back, they were going to talk about this. As resolute as she was, she'd have to shore up her resolve if she was going to do the right thing and stay out of the bedroom.

"What should I say to them?" she asked.

"Let them talk, and you plead ignorance. They'll never know we were up there."

She nodded. "I won't be long."

DEREK HEARD Alyssa close the door behind her, and the apartment fell silent. He sat up slowly, wincing a little. She may have left, but his body hadn't yet gotten that message. He took a deep breath, then let it out slowly, trying to get his scattered thoughts back together where they belonged.

This wasn't like him. Until he'd met Alyssa, the only women he'd slept with were those who knew the score, for whom a one-night stand was good enough, because he never compromised his one woman/one night rule.

So why was Alyssa so different?

She wasn't classically beautiful by any means. She was the kind of woman the average man would find attractive if she came to his attention for some reason, but he might just as easily pass by her. But when she'd turned around that night in the Seattle bar and their eyes had met, something had happened that he hadn't been able to explain.

He still couldn't.

He wasn't one to lose his head over a woman. Ever. Then Alyssa had been standing in her living room a few minutes ago, looking exactly as she had in Seattle—warm and sweet and so incredibly tempting—and before he knew it he had her in his arms and was heading for the bedroom.

He frowned. She was so damned trusting. *Too* trusting. What the hell had she been doing letting him, a total stranger, take her to his room at that Seattle hotel? And what the hell was she doing letting him come to her apartment now? Good God. One of these days she was going to get herself killed.

Derek stood, snagged his shirt from the floor and pulled it on. He grabbed his gun, slid it into the back of his jeans, then snatched up his jacket.

He walked into the living room. He'd been paying no attention before, but now he stopped to look at it. He assumed this apartment, like hers in Seattle, was company-issue, because he didn't think she ever would have chosen to live in a place like this. The soaring ceilings and contemporary architecture were out of step with her eclectic decor. Her sofa looked as if she'd picked it up at a resale shop, and in the dining room were four mismatched chairs around a rich oak table. The pieces of artwork looked like they'd been bought because they'd struck her fancy, not because they might have contributed to a decorating scheme. On almost every flat surface rested photos of friends and family members. One evening in Seattle she'd related the stories behind them. But all of it, in one way or another, was Alyssa through and through.

He glanced at the coffee table and his gaze fell on a folded card. Curious, he picked it up and opened it. It was an invitation to an alumni association event taking place tonight at the Devonshire Hotel for the college Alyssa had attended. Inside the invitation was a separate card noting the recipient of their annual award, which was presented to a former student in recognition of his or her outstanding professional, personal and civic achievements.

Alyssa was receiving the award.

He wasn't the least bit surprised. She excelled at her job, and he knew she spent a good amount of her free time volunteering for various causes. She had a good heart. Too good, really. She was one of those individuals other people took advantage of, yet still she kept on giving. He'd told her once that it didn't sound like much fun to have a job that required her to run herself ragged for demanding rich people, but she'd just smiled and told him that rich people weren't any different than anyone else—they just wanted to know that somebody gave a damn.

Derek sat on the sofa and a memory came to mind. One evening he'd sat on this sofa in Alyssa's Seattle apartment, a bowl of popcorn in his lap and Alyssa's head resting on his shoulder as they'd watched some old movie on TV. She'd fallen asleep. He'd slipped the remote from her hand and turned off the television, then just sat there in the lazy warmth of her apartment, his arm around her, staring at the lush fullness of her mouth and the lamplight playing off the highlights in her hair. After a while he'd carried her to bed and made love to her slowly and completely, and even now he swore he could still hear her moans of pleasure and feel her soft hands clutching his shoulders…

No. Get that out of your mind.

What he'd done in Seattle had been a mistake. To end up half-naked with her today had been an even bigger one, because nothing had changed. He still had a lifestyle that made any kind of relationship out of the question, especially a relationship with a woman like Alyssa. Six months ago he'd had the luxury of a whole week's free time to pretend to be the nice, normal man a woman like her needed, not the globe-hopping mercenary who would only cause her grief.

Currently he had no such luxury. He put the invitation back on the table, his thoughts circling back around to his own job. There were still five congressmen with blackmail material hanging over their heads. Getting sidetracked like this wasn't in the cards, so he needed to get out of there ASAP.

Derek leaned his head against the back of the sofa, feeling the same way he had in Seattle—overcome by the most excruciating push and pull of wanting to stay and needing to go. That thought hammered at him, his mind screaming with indecision. He wasn't used to this. He thought definitively. Acted decisively. And here he was wondering what the hell to do.

No. He knew what to do.

He got up and looked out the window. The two police cars still sat on the street in front of the building. The moment they left, he assumed security would open up the building again and he could get out of here.

With luck, he could leave before Alyssa even got back.

She'd hate him for it, of course, but maybe that was for the best. That way she'd know for sure just how wrong he was for her, and it would make it easier for her simply to go on with her life and forget all about him.

Then he could get back to the business of forgetting all about her.

ALYSSA MET the head of security and a pair of police officers in the penthouse. Once they determined that the apartment was empty, they investigated the premises. With no signs of a break-in and apparently nothing missing, they decided there hadn't been a burglary. And since no one had been home at the time to fire a weapon, the cops decided that the neighbors on the floor below had been mistaken in thinking they'd heard a gunshot. Alyssa told them she'd been in there earlier to clean up a broken vase, the broken pieces of which she'd bagged and left to show the tenant, but she hadn't seen or heard anyone on the premises.

Ultimately they chalked up the broken window to a flaw in its construction coupled with wind and weather conditions that must have caused it to spontaneously shatter. The officers took down Owens's phone number and said they would contact him about the incident to see of he could shed further light on what had happened. Otherwise there was nothing more to investigate. After they left the building. Alyssa told the head of maintenance to get somebody up there right away to clean up the mess and put in a new window, then headed back to her apartment.

Thirty minutes had passed. She came down the hall, picturing Derek as she'd left him, and that awkward feeling overtook her again.

Stand your ground. Ask questions. Get answers.

As she unlocked her door, her heart thumped wildly. When she swung it open, though, she was unprepared for the heavy, pulsing silence that greeted her. She glanced around the living room.

His backpack wasn't where he'd left it.

An ominous feeling came over her. She went into the bedroom. He wasn't there. She didn't see his clothes. She didn't see his gun on the dresser. She called his name softly, even though she already knew the truth.

He was gone.

For at least thirty seconds she stared at her empty apartment, overcome by the strangest feeling that she'd just awakened from a nap and everything that had happened between them had been a dream.

She sat on the bed, thinking back to Seattle, how she'd been drawn in by the mystery that surrounded him, then captivated by his sheer charisma. And he'd been so adept at keeping the focus on her that it hadn't been until afterward that she'd realized just how little he'd revealed about himself. She'd basked in the way he'd been so riveted on her, listening to her talk about her job, her family, her life, then taking hours in bed to discover what made her sigh with pleasure. She spent her life doing things for other people, but Derek had shown her what it felt like to be the center of someone's attention. She'd never been so blissfully ignorant in her life. As it had back then, the most irrational feeling of loss now overcame her.

No. She hadn't lost a thing. In fact, she'd gained something today. Their time in Seattle had felt like an open-ended story with far too many unanswered questions. At least now she knew who he was and had some inkling as to why he'd left. And she also knew that unless she happened to be hanging around a penthouse apartment he was burglarizing in the future, she'd never see him again.

Closing her eyes, she put her hand down on the sheet and swore it still felt warm. When he'd disappeared in Seattle, she'd still been filled with the endorphins of love at first sight, the hope that there'd be an explanation for his disappearance, that his situation would change one day and he'd come back into her life. This time it was worse. This time she'd had her eyes wide open to the dangers and she'd leaped, anyway. She'd always been a quick study, but where Derek was concerned, her brain was slow as molasses.

No more.

She got up from the bed, yanked off the sheets and the pillowcases and tossed them into the clothes hamper. Then she grabbed new linens and made the bed again, tucking in the corners with military precision, taking great care to smooth the comforter back over them until not a single wrinkle remained. Derek had come back into her life and put it into chaos, and it was time she got it straightened out again.

He was gone. Gone as if he'd never even been here. Gone in exactly the way she should have expected—without a word and without a trace. If not for a blown-out window on the twenty-third floor, she could almost make herself believe it had only been a dream.

6

As KEVIN PULLED the van away from the Waterford, Derek reached into the glove compartment, grabbed a pair of sunglasses and slid them on, a welcome relief against the late-afternoon sun. He leaned against the armrest, staring straight ahead, trying to think about the job at hand rather than what had happened in Alyssa's apartment. And he was failing miserably.

"So where are we with the blackmail situation?" Kevin asked.

"Same as before. We're in a holding pattern. Owens should be in Washington any minute and then we'll wait for him to talk. If he does, we'll be back in business again."

Kevin nodded and then drove in silence for a few more minutes. At the next stoplight, he braked to a halt and turned to Derek.

"I saw the blown-out window," Kevin said. "That was in the penthouse, right?"

"Yeah."

"You never did tell me what happened. Was that a gunshot I heard?"

Derek paused. "Yeah."

"Anybody hurt?"

"No."

"I guess that was why the cops showed up."

Derek said nothing.

"You were in that building quite awhile. Is everything okay?"

"Yes," Derek said. "Everything's taken care of."

"The woman?"

"She won't talk. No one will ever know I was in that penthouse."

Derek was absolutely certain of that. He knew Alyssa had believed him when he'd told her who he was and what he was doing there, and she wouldn't say a word, no matter how angry she might be because he'd left her one more time.

He'd left her one more time.

The words reverberated inside his head, sounding so accusatory that an unaccustomed sense of shame welled up inside him.

"You were a long time coming down," Kevin said. "I was afraid—"

"Damn it, I told you everything's fine."

Derek spoke more sharply than he'd intended. Kevin clamped his mouth shut and concentrated on the road ahead of him. After a minute, Derek sighed.

"There's just no need to go into it," he said. "As I told you, everything's taken care of." *The way I take care of everything concerning Alyssa. By walking away.*

Then again, would it have helped the situation if he'd hung around to say goodbye? It would only have caused a scene between them, and in the end that wouldn't have been good for either of them.

Derek's cell phone rang. He pulled it from his

pocket and looked at the Caller ID, then hit the talk button. "Gus? What's up? You should be flying into Washington by now."

"Yeah, I should, shouldn't I?"

Derek didn't like the sound of his friend's voice. "What's happening?"

"Well, it seems there's a band of severe thunderstorms hanging over Washington. I can't land there, so they're not letting me off the ground here."

Damn. Derek looked at his watch. "How long are they estimating it'll take the storm to clear?"

"They aren't. But I saw the weather radar. It could be another hour at least before I can get out of here. You see what I'm saying, Derek? If I make this trip to Washington, I'll miss the rehearsal dinner tonight. You know, the one you swore I'd be back for?"

"Take it easy, Gus."

"Damn it! I knew this was going to happen! What the *hell* am I supposed to tell Sally? She's going to freak out when she hears this!"

Gus wasn't kidding about that. Derek knew Sally. Gus had come clean with her about his past when the two of them had gotten engaged. He hadn't given her any specifics, but she knew the dangerous kind of work he'd done and that Derek had been head of the team. Derek liked Sally a lot, even if she had taken his pilot away from him. Unfortunately she was a tad on the emotional side, and saying she was going to freak out was a huge understatement.

"What have you already told her?" Derek asked.

"I said I skipped the golf game to take care of a client, but I'd be back in plenty of time for the dinner. Now what am I supposed to do?"

Derek blew out a breath. "Call her now. Tell her your client situation has escalated and you have to fly to Washington and you won't be back in time for the dinner tonight." He paused. "Wait. Better yet, call somebody else and have them relay the message to her."

"Why would I do that?"

"The truth? So Sally won't be able to talk you into skipping out on me."

There was a long silence.

"I ought to pull the plug on this whole thing," Gus muttered.

"No. I know I can count on you to get this done for me."

Another silence.

"Gus?"

"Okay! Fine! I'll fly to Washington. But you get your ass to that dinner tonight and smooth things over with Sally. She's going to suspect you're involved in this, anyway. Might as well tell her the truth."

"Don't worry. I'll let her know what's really going on when I get there. I'll tell her you're doing a job for me, that I coerced you into it, and that I told you to lie about it. I'll take the rap for everything."

"Damn right you will." He sighed. "I can't believe this. I can't believe I'm not going to be with her tonight."

"It'll be late when you get to Washington, so you might as well stay put," Derek told him. "Deliver Owens, get a hotel room, then fly back here first thing in the morning. You'll be back in plenty of time for the wedding. That's the important thing, right?"

"I'm leaving before dawn," Gus said. "No way am I taking any more chances that I won't be back in time."

"Good idea."

"I'm still pissed."

"I know you are."

"I have a long memory. I *will* get back at you for this."

"Yeah? I'm still waiting for you to get back at me for setting you up with that transvestite in Copenhagen."

Silence.

"Derek?"

"Yeah?"

"Are you *trying* to dig yourself in deeper?"

Derek smiled. "I'm not sure I could get in any deeper."

"I'm saving up. And believe me. Payback is going to be a *bitch*."

"I don't doubt that." Derek's smile faded. "Seriously, Gus. Don't worry about Sally. I promise you I'll smooth things over, okay?"

Derek hung up with a heavy sigh, wondering if there was any way that this day could get worse.

"So Gus is delayed?" Kevin said.

"Looks that way."

"And you're dealing with his fiancée."

"Uh-huh."

Kevin shook his head sadly. "Man, I wouldn't want to be you right about now."

A wedding rehearsal dinner. Derek could think of

about a thousand places he'd rather be, particularly since he was going to have to deal with an irate bride with murder on her mind.

A COUPLE OF HOURS LATER Derek pulled up to the Courtland Hotel in downtown Dallas. The sun had almost set and the chandelier-lit foyer glowed warmly beyond the brass-trimmed glass doors. He got out of his car and flipped his keys to the valet. The doorman greeted him with a snooty, "Good evening, sir," as he swung the door open.

Derek had been to functions all over the world at hotels that made this one look like a Motel 6, but he'd never grown completely comfortable with those situations. Blending in was never a problem—he'd always been very good at projecting whatever exterior image he needed to. But inside he always felt as if he was coming up short. Given where he came from, that was hardly a surprise.

Derek checked with the front desk and they directed him to the ballroom where the dinner was being held. It was still the cocktail hour, and men in dark suits and women dressed to kill were enjoying drinks and hors d'oeuvres, but there wasn't a damned thing Derek was going to enjoy about this evening—for more than one reason. Even as he faced the unwelcome prospect of having to soothe Sally, he couldn't get his mind off Alyssa.

"Where the *hell* is Gus?"

Derek spun around to see Sally approaching him. *Here we go,* he thought. *Round one. Just pray there's not a knockout punch.*

She looked as she always did—well-dressed, strikingly beautiful and filthy rich. He didn't hold that last one against her, even though she came from a family who could probably buy the entire city of Dallas if they so chose. One of the things Sally liked about Gus was that he didn't give a damn about her money.

"Sally," he said, "you might want to keep your voice down."

"I'm not in much of a mood to keep my voice down."

"Just the same, it'll be better for all concerned if we keep things nice and calm, okay?"

Sally dropped her voice, but anger still rolled through it. "My maid of honor got a call from Gus this afternoon. He told her to pass a message along to me that his client's security situation had escalated and he had to fly to Washington. That's crap, isn't it?"

Leave it to Sally to cut to the chase.

"Not exactly," Derek said. "He is flying to Washington. But he's not taking care of a client. He's taking care of a situation for me."

"I knew it! I *knew* when the other groomsmen saw him leaving with you this afternoon that you were involved in this!"

"Take it easy, Sally. He'll be back in plenty of time for the wedding. He's going to stay over in Washington tonight, then head back to Dallas first thing in the morning."

A waiter came by with a tray of hors d'oeurves. Sally gave the unsuspecting man the evil eye and he scurried off.

She whipped back around. "Fine. But what about tonight? Everybody here knows Gus didn't show up at the golf course this afternoon and now they're really going to wonder what's wrong. I can already hear the gossip!"

"I'm sorry about that. But if it weren't important, I never would have asked him to do it."

"And his wedding isn't important?"

"Of course it is. But I'm dealing with high stakes here. You know the kind of work my team does."

Sally took a few deep breaths. She didn't look the least bit calm, but Derek had to hand it to her. She was trying hard to pull it together. And to avoid killing him.

"Okay," she said tightly. "So what am I supposed to tell everyone?"

"Stick to the story about his client situation. Tell them he had to fly to Washington and that the weather has delayed him, but that he'll be back first thing in the morning. Can you do that?"

"You haven't left me any choice, have you?" She paused. "Either of you."

"Listen to me, Sally. Gus agreed to do this job for me for one reason only. Because I swore to him that I'd have him back in time to be here tonight. If you want to blame somebody, blame me, not him."

"I blame both of you. It hasn't changed, has it? He's still ready to drop everything for the sake of the team."

"He dropped everything to help out an old friend, who had to twist his arm to get him to do it."

"Apparently his loyalty isn't to me. It's to you."

"He has loyalty to everyone he loves. You know that."

Sally closed her eyes with a sigh.

"And he loves you," Derek said.

Her lids flew open. "He has a fine way of show-ing it."

"He doesn't want to be part of the team anymore. A year ago I tried my damnedest to hang on to him, but it turned out that you were what he wanted. I couldn't compete with you. I couldn't even play in the same ballpark."

Sally eyed him, her lips still tight with irritation.

"I know how important this is. And it's my fault he's not here. He gave in because he's a loyal guy, but even then he never would have done it if he thought there was a chance that he'd miss more than a round of golf. Just please don't take it out on him."

She bowed her head in resignation, then looked back up at Derek. "You know, planning a wedding is a pain in the ass. I anticipated that some things might go wrong. But this wasn't one of them."

"But think what a good story it'll make someday."

She rolled her eyes. "Right."

"You know. In about ten years."

She pursed her lips.

"Twenty?"

"Hey, I'm trying to stay mad at Gus here. You're not helping."

"So you're not mad at him?"

"Hell, no! I love him too much to stay mad at him!" She huffed with frustration. "Though I'm not ruling out a little creative punishment. Is it tacky to withhold sex on your wedding night?"

Derek smiled. Gus was in for it. This woman was going to keep him hopping for the rest of his life.

Then Sally's brows pulled together with concern. "Tell me exactly what he's doing, Derek. He's safe, isn't he?"

"All he's doing is transporting some cargo to Washington. That cargo is handcuffed, and big, ugly men are standing over him with firearms. Gus is just flying the plane."

"You wouldn't be lying to me about that, would you?"

"Okay. You've got me. The men with firearms really aren't all that ugly."

Sally cracked a reluctant smile and shook her head.

"I swear he's safe," Derek said. "And he'll be back first thing in the morning."

"You know if he's not, you're going to have to deal with me."

"And that strikes fear in my heart, believe me. I'll definitely have him to the church on time."

Sally was still unhappy, not because she was angry with Gus, but because the man she loved was a thousand miles away on a very important night. And he knew Gus was just as unhappy to be away from her.

Just then, other members of the wedding party came up beside them. Sally introduced them to Derek. Then she did a credible job of passing on to them the story Gus had told her, telling them that one of the companies he did security for had a break-in, so he had to fly there to investigate. And because of weather problems, he hadn't been able to make it back. Everyone in the wedding party seemed relatively satisfied with the explanation, and since Sally wasn't as distraught as she had been earlier, they took her lead and brushed it off, too.

Before dinner was served, Sally rose to explain Gus's absence to the rest of the guests. As she spoke, a low hum of suspicion rose in the room. But Sally got through the explanation with composure and even a little bit of wit about the situation. Once dinner was served and everyone had a few more drinks, a party atmosphere settled over the ballroom and Derek could tell that everything was going to be all right.

At least Gus was covered.

By this time tomorrow Gus would be married. He'd be on a plane heading for a Caribbean island with his new wife, where they would have two weeks of total relaxation before they started their new life together.

Together.

Just that word conjured up images of things Derek had never made a priority in his life, and marriage topped that list. Up to now, his only reaction to Gus's leaving the team was distress that he was going to be without his right-hand man. But now, looking around this room at the friends and family gathered to celebrate Gus's wedding, another feeling inched its way in. Envy. And Derek knew why.

Because of Alyssa.

Seeing her again had stirred up all kinds of feelings he shouldn't be having. The very idea that they could ever have any kind of relationship was laughable when their lives were so vastly different. In Seattle, Alyssa had talked about wanting a family one day that was as warm and close as hers was. Of course, she'd thought she was talking to a man who had the capacity to give her that. She'd had no idea he barely knew the meaning of the word "family" and wouldn't have the first clue how to be part of one.

The waiters served dinner, some gourmet thing that Derek couldn't even identify piled high on the plate. He wasn't much for making idle conversation under the best of circumstances, but doing it over dinner with the people at this table was excruciating. He just wanted out of here. He checked his watch, wondering how soon he could leave without offending Sally. He decided he'd stay until dessert was served and then slip out.

Oh, hell. What good would leaving do? Being alone would only make thoughts of Alyssa loom even larger in his mind than they did right now.

This was ridiculous. What was the *matter* with him?

Derek had always prided himself on his logical, rational approach to life. In his business, emotion only got in the way. But right now he felt as if logic and rationality had completely deserted him.

He wanted to see her again.

You're nuts. She'll slam the door in your face. And rightly so.

She'd saved him from certain disaster this afternoon by taking him to her apartment, trusting him one more time, and he'd thanked her by disappearing without a trace. He might want to see her again, but the chances of that feeling being mutual were less than zero. She may have been on the verge of welcoming him into her bed this afternoon, but they'd been in the middle of an emotionally charged situation. Once she'd returned to her apartment this afternoon to find him gone, she'd undoubtedly written him off for good. It wouldn't take three strikes for her to call him out. He had no doubt that two was plenty.

Forget her. It was over when you walked out the door this afternoon. You made a clean break. Leave it that way and get on with your life.

He sat straight and picked up his knife and fork. After determining that there was some beef beneath the pile of stuff on his plate, he managed to eat a little of it. He chatted with the people at the table even though he had to choke out the words. He smiled appropriately when other people talked. But if his life depended on remembering any of their names or a single word anyone had spoken, he'd be a dead man.

Instead his thoughts drifted to Alyssa again. He saw her at the Devonshire Hotel right now, receiving that alumni award. No doubt she deserved it. No doubt she'd accept it humbly. And no doubt she'd look beautiful doing it.

If only he could be there instead of here.

Right. And the moment she saw him she'd call hotel security and have him dragged off the premises.

He dropped his silverware to his plate and pushed the dish away. The feeling of wanting to see her, *needing* to see her, grew stronger with every moment that passed, and by the time the waiters came around with trays of desserts, he was burning with it. It wasn't rational. It wasn't reasonable.

And it wouldn't go away.

A waiter set the dessert in front of him. Derek looked down at it, then lifted his gaze to glance around the room, at the smiling faces of family and friends celebrating one of life's biggest events. And suddenly everything about it seemed unreal. Dreamlike. As if he was an outsider looking in.

It's because these people have real lives, and you don't.

The feeling of being alone in the world was nothing new to Derek. But tonight, in this place, that feeling was suddenly magnified ten times over.

He didn't know what he was going to say to Alyssa. All he knew was that he had to see her again.

7

ALYSSA HAD ALWAYS loved the Devonshire Hotel, a grand old turn-of-the-century building that defined elegance itself. It smelled of fine wood and dripped with chandeliers, and the staff filtered through its majestic spaces with understated grace. Under normal circumstances, she'd be enjoying the atmosphere. Tonight, though, she was nothing but a bundle of nerves.

She sat with her sister and her parents at one of three dozen candlelit tables in the Grand Ballroom. A long, leisurely dinner had been served and now they were waiting for the program to begin. She clasped her hands together, only to realize they were sweating. She wiped them surreptitiously on a cocktail napkin.

"Nervous?" Kim asked.

"I'm not crazy about public speaking," Alyssa said quietly.

"Just get up there, accept the award, thank the little people and step down."

"If only it were as simple as that." She took a deep, calming breath, which did nothing to calm her at all. "I *hate* this."

"Yeah, but it never shows. You always make stuff like this look easy."

A few minutes later the president of the alumni association took the stage and Alyssa applauded with the rest of the crowd. As the woman began the opening speech of the evening, Alyssa tried to focus on what she was saying, but concentration came with difficulty right about now, and not just because of her nervousness. What should have been a red-letter night for her was overshadowed by thoughts of the man who'd come into her life this day and upset it one more time.

She glanced across the table at her mother and father. Her mother had bought a new dress for the occasion, one that she'd reported to Alyssa had cost a hundred and forty-nine dollars. But she'd said she didn't care about that. This was a special evening. Alyssa didn't think her mother had spent over fifty dollars for a dress in her entire life. And her father had willingly put on a suit. For a man who spent his days in a mechanic's garage and thought ties ranked right up there with hangmen's nooses, it was a big sacrifice.

This was as much a night for them as it was for her, a night to get excited over one of their children's accomplishments. So it was time to get her head back into the game and to remind herself what was important. And it wasn't a man who didn't think twice about lying *or* leaving.

Alyssa endured the president's speech about the association's accomplishments over the past year, complete with a lengthy and excruciatingly boring

PowerPoint presentation. By the time she got around to announcing the award, Alyssa was a basket case.

Finally she heard her name called, then applause. She rose from her chair and went to the front of the room, thanked the president and went to the podium. As she laid her note card in front of her, her hands were shaking.

She began to speak. She didn't have that much prepared to say, but every moment still seemed an hour long. She remembered the public-speaking workshop she'd taken, otherwise known as The Class From Hell, that had taught her to make eye contact with as many people in the audience as she could. She forced her gaze around the room.

And that was when she saw Derek.

He stood at the back of the room, leaning against the wall, wearing a dark suit, blue shirt, conservative tie. She'd never seen him in anything but jeans before, so at first she told herself it couldn't be him. Then she looked at his stance, the angle of his chin, the intensity of his gaze even at this distance, and she told herself it couldn't be anyone else. At the mere sight of him, every bone in her body seemed to melt.

His eyes locked onto hers and for a moment she didn't speak. Actually it must have been several moments, because the crowd began to murmur and several people turned to look toward the back of the room.

Alyssa cleared her throat and continued, suddenly feeling flushed and disoriented. She deliberately avoided looking in his direction, wrapping up her speech quickly and then leaving the stage to another round of applause. As she made her way back to her table, she told herself that maybe nobody had noticed her momentary confusion.

"Who's the guy?" Kim whispered.

"What guy?"

"Come on, Alyssa. The one standing at the back of the room who tied your tongue into a knot."

Oh, *God*. If Kim had noticed, then probably everyone had.

"Uh, no one," she stammered. "Just…just someone I thought I knew."

"So you don't know him?"

"No. I don't."

Kim looked over her shoulder. "Well, you're getting ready to. He's coming this way."

Alyssa whipped around. With the program over, people were coming to their feet and heading to the buffet line for dessert and champagne. Derek was weaving in and out of the crowd, circling around tables, heading in her direction.

She set the plaque she'd received on the table. "I'll be back in a minute," she told Kim.

"Alyssa, wait! Where are you going?"

She ignored her sister and kept walking, edging her way around people as she headed for the door. She had no idea why he was here, and she didn't want to find out. For all her ability to keep her cool, Derek was the one person who just might make her lose it.

"Alyssa."

She lengthened her strides.

"Alyssa!"

He caught her arm and she was forced to stop or

make a scene. She spoke under her breath. "How did you know I was here?"

"I saw the invitation on your coffee table."

"Why do you keep doing this to me?"

"What?"

"This coming-and-going thing. I can't take any more of it."

"Once the coast was clear this afternoon, I had to get out of that building. I thought you understood that."

"You were perfectly safe in my apartment."

"I don't take chances."

She looked at him plaintively. "What do you want from me?"

"I just want to talk."

"You didn't have to come here tonight for that. You know where I live."

"As if you'd let me back into your apartment."

"How about letting me into yours?"

"What?"

"I don't even know where you live, Derek. I'm not even certain we live in the same *country*. Isn't it strange that after everything that has happened between us, I still don't know who you really are?"

"All I want to do is talk. Is that really such a big deal?"

"Yes. Because if it's anything like this afternoon, before I know it, we won't be talking anymore."

He raised an eyebrow. "Would that really be so awful?"

"Stop it."

"Alyssa—"

"Will you please just go away and leave me alone?"

He narrowed his eyes. "Is that what you really want?"

God, no. She wanted him to stay. She wanted that man she knew in Seattle back again. But he didn't seem to exist anymore, and his track record for sticking around, whoever he happened to be, left a lot to be desired.

She couldn't take this anymore. She just couldn't. She needed to get off this roller coaster and she needed to get off it *now*.

"Yes," she said. "That's what I want."

"Okay," he said. "I'll leave."

But instead of turning around and walking away, he took a step toward her, standing so close she had to tilt her head back to meet his eyes.

"Just tell me one thing first," he said.

"What?"

"Tell me when you were on that stage tonight and you looked up to see me standing there, that you weren't glad to see me. Tell me that, and I'll leave right now."

She swallowed hard, knowing her expression was giving her away but she was unable to stop him from reading the truth on her face. Hell, yes, she'd been glad to see him, because her heart was still looking at him through those rose-colored glasses, the ones she'd worn for an entire week in Seattle and should have smashed into a million tiny pieces.

No. Don't let him do this to you. Don't you dare let him do it—

"Oh, God," she said.

"What?"

She glanced over his shoulder. "My sister and my parents are coming this way."

Derek backed away from her, turning around just as Kim reached him. She gave him an appreciative once-over, which she topped off with a great big smile.

"Hi, there," she said. "I'm Alyssa's sister, Kim."

Derek returned her smile. "Hi, Kim. I'm Derek Stafford."

Alyssa froze, praying that somehow her sister would get a case of sudden amnesia where that name was concerned.

No such luck.

Kim's eyebrows shot up, her eyes widening with surprise, and she opened her mouth to say something. Alyssa instantly gave her a look of warning and she clamped it shut again. Derek introduced himself to Alyssa's father and mother.

"It's a pleasure to meet you," her mother said. "So how do you and Alyssa know each other?"

"We met in Seattle," Derek said.

She turned to Alyssa. "You never told us you were seeing someone in Seattle."

"Derek and I were just friends."

"Good friends," Derek said. "I just happened to be able to make it tonight at the last minute." He looked at Alyssa. "And I'm really glad I did."

Her mother beamed at him. Clearly she saw a relationship in the future for her workaholic daughter, which of course would lead to marriage and grandchildren.

"Of course you'll join us for dessert and champagne in the ballroom," she said, "won't you?"

"I'd love to," he said.

And Alyssa wanted to kill him.

"THAT WAS SHAMELESS," Alyssa whispered to him as they stood in the buffet line waiting for dessert and champagne. "You knew I wouldn't say anything."

"Uh-huh," he whispered back. "Shamelessness can be very effective."

Her parents and sister stood with them in line. Jim Ballard was a big, friendly looking man, mostly bald, with just the slightest shadow of grease beneath his fingernails, the kind that became permanent when a man spent every day working underneath a car. Marie was a slight woman with prematurely graying hair and a smile that said the first time she met someone was the last time they were a stranger.

Alyssa had talked about her parents a lot in Seattle, and he remembered thinking that it all sounded very nice, but she had to be exaggerating their virtues at least a little bit. Now that he'd met them in person, though, he had to say that at least they seemed genuine. Still, Derek wasn't sure if he could take them at face value or not. In his experience, if somebody seemed too good to be true, they probably were.

Kim was another story. If he remembered right, she was a few years older than Alyssa, and Alyssa had told him that outside of their sisterly squabbles as children, they'd always gotten along well. But Kim wasn't speaking at all now, merely looking at him with the kind of suspicion that made him wonder if she knew more about him than she was letting on.

Conversation came easily with her parents,

though, and that was mostly because they talked so freely about Alyssa.

"She works at one of Lawrence Teague's properties, you know," Marie said. "He's a very important man."

"Real-estate entrepreneur," Jim said. "Big bucks. Owns luxury buildings all across the country."

"Yes," Derek said. "Alyssa told me about him in Seattle."

"Alyssa is practically indispensable at the Dallas property," Marie said. "The tenants love her."

"If the tenants don't stay, Teague doesn't make money. He's got Alyssa to thank for that."

Alyssa winced. "Mom, Dad, you're laying it on a little thick."

"Hell we are," Jim said, then looked at Derek. "They don't hand out awards like the one she got tonight for nothing, you know."

Derek smiled. "I know."

Several people came up to Alyssa to congratulate her, and her parents beamed with delight. One thing was certain, if nothing else—they were proud of their daughter.

They took their food and drinks back to the table. Derek continued to talk to Jim and Marie, but the whole time his attention was focused on Alyssa. Very nonchalantly, he slipped his hand beneath the table and rested it just above her knee. Out of the corner of his eye, he saw her shoot him a subtle look of surprise, but he ignored it, choosing instead to rub his thumb back and forth against the bare skin there, softly and casually, as if touching her like this was the most natural thing in the world.

Yes, he was being shameless all over again. But he didn't care. If any opportunity to get his hands on Alyssa presented itself, he was going to take it.

During a lull in the conversation when her well-wishers had tapered off and her parents' attention was directed somewhere else, Alyssa leaned toward him.

"What do you think you're doing?" she whispered.

He could smell the soft notes of her floral perfume, almost feel her breath on his cheek. If she truly wanted him to stop touching her, she'd just made a tactical error by leaning in so close.

"What am I doing?" he repeated. "I'm touching you the only way I can in polite company." He paused. "And wishing we weren't in polite company."

Her cheeks immediately flushed pink, her eyes widening, and for a moment he was sure she was going to pull away from him. Instead she touched her tongue to her lower lip, her gaze glued to his.

"Shameless," she whispered.

"I'm still not denying that."

"You had your chance this afternoon."

"Was that my last one?"

She slid her hand beneath the table and took hold of his, presumably to make him stop. But as she pressed her hand over his on her thigh, she blinked dreamily, and her chest rose and fell with a deep, silent breath.

In that moment he knew just how conflicted she felt. She couldn't stop herself from wanting him any more than he could stop himself from wanting her, and it gave him hope that maybe he hadn't completely screwed this up after all. He wasn't laboring under any delusions that she'd suddenly decided to forgive him, but at least she seemed willing to give him a chance.

"So, Derek," Jim said, "do you live here in Dallas?"

"Uh…no. I'm just here on business."

"So where are you from?"

He'd known these kinds of questions could come up, but now, as he poised himself to lie, his heart began to beat a little harder, setting his nerves on edge. Of course, the first scenario that came to mind was the one he'd told Alyssa in Seattle. It was easy and familiar and…

And Alyssa could quote it right along with him.

"Kansas City," he said.

"Is that Kansas City, Kansas, or Kansas City, Missouri?"

"Missouri," he said, then quickly changed the subject. "Alyssa told me you're a mechanic."

"Yep. I worked at a garage here in Dallas for several years. Then I opened my own shop."

"It's always nice to be the boss," Derek said.

"Yeah, but it's a hassle, too. I had these two girls to support, though, so more money was a welcome thing." He leaned closer to Derek. "When the time comes, have boys. They're one hell of a lot cheaper. The prom dresses alone will put you in the poorhouse."

That earned him a slap on the arm and an admonishing glare from Marie. "Those dresses were worth every penny," she told Derek. "The girls both looked beautiful."

"Can't even imagine what the weddings are going to run me," Jim grumbled. "This one's engaged," he said, pointing to Kim. Then he nodded toward Alyssa. "And you can bet this one won't be far behind."

Marie rolled her eyes. "Don't listen to him. He can't wait to play father of the bride."

She slid her hand inside the crook of her husband's elbow and gave him a smile, and Derek could tell the two of them probably hadn't had a real argument in years.

If ever.

Suddenly it struck him just how unwarranted his suspicion had been. These two were the real thing. People who were exactly as they appeared to be— hardworking, decent people devoted to their family. They loved their children, and they loved each other. Alyssa had told him that her mother had always been the Girl Scout leader or homeroom mother, a woman who'd cooked dinner every evening and baked cookies and shuttled Alyssa and her sister and their friends all over town. And she'd done it all, in addition to working a full-time job during most of those years, because she'd had the unending support of her husband. Derek had encountered so few of these kinds of people in his life that just sitting here talking to them seemed surreal.

"So, Derek," Jim said, "what line of work are you in?"

Derek could spout the details about this particular alias if somebody shook him awake from a dead sleep, but now, for some reason, when he started to speak, he couldn't make the words come out.

Just say it. You're a security analyst for Primus Engineering, a manufacturing company in Kansas City.

He glanced over to find Alyssa staring at him with nervous expectation, the beats of silence mounting as he left the question unanswered. He knew she'd never call him in a lie no matter how many he piled on top of each other.

Suddenly he felt ashamed of that.

He flicked his gaze back to her parents. They were so easy to lie to, just as Alyssa had been, because there wasn't a jaded or suspicious bone in their bodies. Jim and Marie clearly loved their daughter. They were treating him as if he were already part of the family just by virtue of the fact that he was a friend of Alyssa's. They had no reason to think he wasn't every bit as genuine as they were.

He didn't remember a time in his life when words had come hard to him. His livelihood relied on his ability to talk himself into and out of sticky situations, but suddenly he couldn't seem to answer a simple question with a simple lie.

But the truth wasn't an option, either.

He made a play of checking his watch. "You know, I just remembered a phone call I have to make. Would you excuse me for just a minute?"

He eased away from Alyssa, stood and walked out of the ballroom, overcome by the most uncanny feeling that while he had a dozen aliases to fall back on, somewhere along the way he'd lost himself.

8

ALYSSA WATCHED as Derek walked out the door, trying to come to grips with the fact that he'd risen so abruptly from the table.

And disappeared again.

No. He's making a phone call. That's all. Nothing to worry about.

She kept telling herself that, but still that familiar sinking feeling overcame her again, that same terrible sensation she'd had in her apartment this afternoon. And in Seattle six months ago. The one that told her he wasn't gone for a few minutes, but for good.

But how could that be? Hadn't he told her when he'd sat down here that he'd do anything to be with her tonight? Hadn't he been touching her as if he couldn't wait to get her alone again?

Stop worrying. He's simply got some business to take care of. That's all.

"Hey, Alyssa," Kim said, "you need more champagne."

"I think I've had enough."

But Kim was already on her feet. "No. I can tell. You need more." She looked over at their parents. "Back in a minute."

Kim practically yanked Alyssa out of her chair and dragged her to the bar. She grabbed two more glasses of champagne and put one of them in Alyssa's hand. Then she leaned in and spoke quietly.

"So, tell me. Is that really him? The guy from Seattle?"

Damn. The last thing Alyssa wanted was the third degree from her sister. Why had she even told Kim about Derek in the first place?

"Yes," she admitted. "That's really him."

"How bizarre is that?" Kim said. "I mean, we were just talking about him today."

"Yeah."

"So what was the deal? Why did he tell you all those lies?"

"Please, Kim, I don't want to talk about that right now."

"And then all of the sudden he shows up here tonight. How did that come about?"

"Kim—"

"I mean, how did he even know you were going to be here? Did you know *he* was going to be here? It didn't look like it to me. There you were, right in the middle of your speech, and all of sudden—"

"Kim—stop."

"No. Don't you dare duck this. You have *got* to tell me what's going on here."

Alyssa sighed. "You wouldn't believe me if I told you."

"Try me."

"He could be back any minute."

"If he comes back, I'll shut up. Talk to me until then."

Finally, Alyssa relented and gave Kim the *Reader's Digest* version of what had happened today, leaving out the part about how they'd almost made love. She didn't want her sister—she didn't want *anyone*—to know just how brainless she became whenever Derek was around.

When she finished, Kim gaped at her. "You have got to be kidding. He's a *spy*?"

"Not exactly, but that's close."

"This is really wild. So what's his real name?"

"I don't know."

"Where does he live?"

She sighed. "I don't know that, either."

"Does he plan on telling you anytime soon?"

"He says his job depends on his anonymity."

"That sounds fishy. Like he's married and lying about it or something. Are you sure he's who he says he is?"

"Yes. I overheard enough to know that he really does work for the government."

"Wow."

"Please don't say anything to anyone about all this. No matter how I feel about Derek, it's something nobody should know."

"My lips are sealed. What else do you know about him?"

"Next to nothing."

"Okay. So why did he come here tonight?"

Alyssa frowned. "I'm not completely sure about that, either."

Kim sighed with frustration. "Well, if nothing else,

at least now I know why you were obsessed. He's *gorgeous*."

"Yeah," Alyssa said weakly. "I know."

"Well, hello there, Alice!"

At the sound of the booming voice, Alyssa turned to see a man standing behind her. Tall. Blond. Obnoxious. The most conceited, self-important man she'd ever met.

No. It couldn't be. Tom the car salesman. What was *he* doing here?

"The name is Alyssa," she told him.

"Oh, yeah, right," Tom said. "Hey, I'm surprised to see you here tonight. Didn't know you were getting an award. Imagine that."

"I believe it was mentioned in the invitation."

"Hell, I didn't pay attention to that. I just came for the party. I didn't even know we went to the same college."

"We talked about it at lunch today."

"Hmm. Must have missed that."

"I don't think I've ever seen you at alumni association meetings," Alyssa said.

"Just joined. Got to thinking it'd be good for networking. I'm already the top salesman at my company, but I've always got room for a few more dollars. I sell luxury cars, you know."

Yeah. She knew.

"Kim," Alyssa said, turning to her sister with a tight smile, "this is Tom. You know, the man you arranged for me to have lunch with today. Tom, this is my sister, Kim."

"Oh, yeah. Jeff's girl, right?"

"Uh, right," Kim said.

"Jeff's a good guy. Drives a Toyota—but, hey, am I holding that against him?"

Kim just stood there, shell-shocked.

Tom leaned in close and gave Alyssa a suggestive look. "Hey, Alice, the party's winding down. How about you and I take that spin in my Beemer I promised you? Got a new CD changer. Top of the line." He leaned back and looked down at her feet. "You'll have to take off the heels, though. They gouge the carpet."

Alyssa turned slowly to look at her sister, who stared back at her with an expression that said, *I'm sorry. I am so, so sorry. I'll never set you up on a blind date again. Thank you for not killing me.*

"I'm afraid not," Alyssa said. "I have plans this evening."

"How about tomorrow?"

"I have plans then, too."

Tom edged in closer. "Might want to cancel those plans, Alice. Not every day you get to ride in a sixty-thousand-dollar vehicle with a man who really knows how to take those corners."

Alyssa was dumbstruck. This guy couldn't be for real. He just *couldn't.*

"Alyssa," Kim said, "I need to go to the ladies' room. You have to go with me."

"Huh?" Her mouth was still agape at his last statement.

"Yeah. You know the rule. Women have to go in pairs." She turned to Tom. "That's a fact, you know. The National Association of Public Restrooms is lobbying Congress to make it a law."

For once, Tom was speechless.

"It's been a real pleasure, Tim," Kim said. "But we gotta go."

Kim lifted the untouched glass of champagne from Alyssa's hand, deposited both of their glasses on a nearby table, then grabbed Alyssa by the arm and hustled her toward the door of the ballroom. Once they were in the hall, they stood against the wall and then Kim leaned over to peer back into the room.

"He's not following us, is he?" Alyssa said.

"No. He's cornered some other woman, poor thing." Kim turned back to Alyssa. "Say thank you."

"For what? Setting me up with *him?*"

"For the fact that I recognized the error of my ways and rescued you from the jaws of boredom."

"Now you can see why lunch with him was such a joy."

"Uh-huh. Your disappearing spy is looking better all the time."

Derek. Where was he?

Alyssa went to the door of the ballroom and looked inside. He wasn't at the table where they'd been sitting. Glancing around, she didn't see him anywhere in the room.

Kim checked her watch and a knowing look came over her face. "He's been gone awhile. Sure he's just making a phone call?"

Alyssa read the subtext of Kim's question loud and clear. "I don't know."

"Think maybe you ought to go find out?"

"I really don't care."

"Oh, *please!* I sat at that table for half an hour

watching you watching him when you didn't think he was watching you. That was a lot of watching going on. You're a goner over that guy. It's probably going to get you in a whole lot of trouble, but it's the truth. Don't even try to deny it."

Alyssa closed her eyes. Was she that transparent? The answer was yes.

"I'll be back in a minute," she told Kim.

Alyssa walked to the lobby of the hotel. A quick glance around told her he wasn't there. She peeked into the lounge, then the restaurant, then the elevator lobby, growing progressively uneasier. He had to be here somewhere. He had to be. Because the only alternative was that he'd disappeared without a trace one more time.

Surely he hadn't done that.

But this wasn't a big hotel. If he were here, wouldn't she have seen him?

Her stomach knotted with apprehension, she went to the concierge desk. The man behind the counter looked up. "Yes, ma'am? May I help you?"

"Did you happen to see a man in the lobby in the last five or ten minutes? Tall, early thirties, dark hair, dark suit, blue shirt…"

She didn't know how else to describe Derek, except maybe *strikingly handsome* and *sexy as hell*. But even with her vague description, the man nodded.

"Yes, ma'am. I saw him."

Her heart skipped. "Where is he?"

"He left the hotel a few minutes ago."

Stunned, Alyssa just stood there, her knotted stomach feeling as if it had plunged right through the floor. She couldn't believe it. Just like that, he was gone. And she didn't have a clue where to find him.

Not that he wanted to be found.

She rested her hand on the counter for several seconds, not completely sure her knees would hold her up. This couldn't be happening. There was no *way* he could have done this to her again. She gritted her teeth for a moment, then swallowed hard. Tears burned behind her eyes and she blinked several times to keep them at bay.

"Ma'am?" the man said. "Are you all right?"

"Yes," she said, her voice choked. "Yes, of course. Thank you for the information."

She walked away from the desk, hoping anger would take over in a moment. That was about the only thing that would erase the humiliation and the sorrow she felt at pouring so many of her hopes into a man who would treat her like this.

"Ma'am?" the concierge said.

She turned back.

"You wouldn't happen to be Alyssa Ballard, would you?"

She stepped back to the desk. "Yes, I am."

"I was just heading into the ballroom with this. The gentleman left it for you."

He handed Alyssa a piece of hotel stationery, folded twice. She opened it and saw an address: 4322 Forest Lane, Apartment 212, Dallas, Texas.

9

MAYBE IT'LL BE OKAY. Maybe she won't come. Maybe she'll toss your address in the trash, and that'll be that.

Derek sat in his living room, the TV turned on but muted, staring at the screen but comprehending nothing.

What the *hell* had he just done?

He didn't want Alyssa here. He didn't want any woman here. The moment she knew where he lived, he no longer had the power to walk away without a trace, which meant he lost control of the situation.

What was the *matter* with him?

He hit the mute button and brought back the sound on the TV. He ran the dial. An infomercial for an ab machine. A talk show. A sitcom rerun. He clicked the TV off again and tossed the remote to the coffee table.

Silence. It was so damned *quiet*.

He looked at his dining room table. Suddenly it struck him how pointless it was even to have one when dinner in his apartment generally consisted of take-out food or a TV dinner in front of a ballgame. Glancing into his kitchen, he had the same kind of revelation about his refrigerator. Another pointless item. Stocking it with food made no sense, because he was never around long enough to eat it before it went bad.

Thank God, Pizza Hut delivered.

He looked around his apartment, at the cheap furniture, the bare walls. This place was ugly as hell. But what was the point of spending any money or making any effort to spruce it up when he was here maybe two or three days out of every month? He couldn't even have a dog to keep him company. Who would take care of him when he was out of town? Hell, forget pets. Plants were even out of the question.

He thought about Alyssa's apartment. So warm. So inviting.

And there were all those photographs.

The few family photos Derek had were in a box in his bedroom closet, and he hadn't looked at them in years. He didn't even know why he kept them. People like Alyssa displayed photos because it made them feel good to have reminders of family members in their midst. And after meeting her family, he knew why.

There was a reason his were in the closet.

Alyssa had had a charmed childhood, with a family that was there for her every step of the way. It was why she'd turned into such an incredible woman. Sweet and sociable in public, hot and wild in private. Smart and capable at all times. Enough independence to be intriguing, enough vulnerability to soften any sharp edges. Not that she had many of those. Alyssa was the kind of woman who could float into a room and make everyone in it feel better than they had before she entered it. Being with her made him feel things he'd never felt before, and every once in a while he'd experience flashes of what it might be like to have someone like her to come home to.

Home. He barely knew the meaning of the word.

Alyssa was a woman who stood on bedrock, while he'd never felt anything but sand beneath his feet. That was the way his life still was—built on shifting ground, putting him in one city today, another tomorrow, with no permanence at all. Which meant he had absolutely nothing to offer a woman like her. That week in Seattle, though, it was as if she'd crawled right inside him, touching him in a way no woman had before. If only he could bring that week back and have that be his reality....

Damn it, he hated this. He hated sitting in the silence of this apartment and letting these thoughts take over, forcing him to admit just how solitary and transient his life really was.

He rubbed his eyes with the heels of his hands, then let out a heavy sigh. He'd lied to himself. It wasn't that he didn't want her here. It was that if she came here, she'd learn soon enough just how wrong he was for her and she'd be gone. It was one thing for him to be the one who left. But it was another thing for him to feel that touch of hope, then watch her walk away from him.

It would be better if she never came here at all.

He looked at his watch and felt relief. An hour had passed. If she were coming tonight, she'd have been here by now.

That was when he heard a knock at his door.

ALYSSA STOOD outside the apartment, her heart pounding, telling herself that this was a mistake, that she was only giving him the opportunity to hurt her one more time. Everything about their relationship had been two steps forward and one step back, and she'd already given him the benefit of too many doubts. But still, for some reason, she was driven to see this through to the end.

Whatever the end turned out to be.

She didn't hear anything inside the apartment and for a minute she wondered if he was home. Then the door swung open and she met Derek face-to-face once again.

His feet were bare and he wore a pair of jeans, along with the dress shirt he'd worn earlier in the evening, unbuttoned down the front with the cuffs hanging loose. It was late, and some of the usual sharpness of his gaze had mellowed into a sleepy relaxation that made him look even sexier than usual. He stood motionless, staring at her.

"Alyssa?"

"You look surprised to see me."

"I am."

"You gave me your address. What did you expect me to do with it?"

He paused several beats, regarding her with a wariness she didn't understand. "I expected you to toss it into the nearest trash can."

"Is that what you wanted me to do?"

Slowly his expression changed. He looked her up and down, his gaze skimming her body. Then he reached for her hand, pulled her inside his apartment and shut the door. He took a step toward her. She instinctively moved away, her back grazing the wall. He stared down at her suggestively.

"What I want," he said, "is to finish what we started this afternoon."

Even as a hot flush of sexual awareness swept through her, Alyssa heard warning bells. In Seattle, he'd looked at her like this a hundred times, but so much more had been beneath that expression— warmth, wit, and what had seemed like a genuine desire to please her. But she saw none of that now. Instead he stared at her with the seductive but vacant expression of a man who wanted sex and nothing else, making her feel as if everything between them had never been.

"What happened to just wanting to talk?" she said.

"Come on, Lys. You know talking only gets in the way of what both of us really want."

"Both of us?"

"Yes. Both of us. You want it, or you wouldn't be here."

To say she didn't want him would have been a lie. But to say she wanted nothing more than sex would be an even bigger one.

"Sure," she said. "We can have sex. Just answer one question for me."

He gave her a sly smile. "Sure, sweetheart. Anything."

"What happened to the man I knew in Seattle?"

He leaned away, his smile evaporating. "He doesn't exist."

"He seemed pretty real to me."

"You mean, the man I made up?" He made a scoffing noise. "You're living in a dreamworld."

"Are you sure about that?"

"I'm a professional liar. You should know that by now."

"You can only lie for so long before the truth comes out."

"I don't know what you're talking about."

"I think the man I knew in Seattle was the real one. I'm not sure who I'm talking to now."

"I've got news for you, Alyssa. You haven't got a clue who I am."

"Maybe that's what we need to talk about."

He stared at her a long time. She sensed a myriad of emotions swirling just beneath the surface, but then his face settled into an expression of total disinterest.

"This was a mistake," he said. "I think it would be best if you just left."

With that, he turned around and walked into his living room. He sat on the sofa, picked up the remote and flipped on the TV, then put his feet up on the coffee table. Pointedly ignoring her, he acted as if she'd already walked out the door.

Alyssa stared at him in disbelief. He'd given her his address and now he was telling her to leave? How could he *do* this to her?

Tears came to her eyes and she fought to blink them away. She shouldn't have come here. He'd yanked her around six months ago and now she was letting him do it again. What kind of masochist was she?

She needed to get out of there. She needed to turn around and leave and never set foot anywhere near this man again. In lieu of her company, he seemed perfectly content to sit inside these four bare walls with nothing but a television to keep him company.

She didn't know how he could stand to exist that way.

Her gaze took in her surroundings. His apartment was neat and clean but unadorned with anything singular or personal. A sofa sat along one wall, a coffee table in front of it, the space lit by a single floor lamp. The television sat on a cheap walnut veneer stand. The dining room held a table and four chairs, with Derek's suit coat and tie resting on the back of one of them. The walls were blank. No art, no photos, no decorative items at all. On a desk on the opposite wall in the living room, though, sat enough computer equipment to run Mission Control.

It was cold. Uninviting. A place designed to sustain life but not live it.

She glanced back at Derek. His gaze flicked to her, then moved away again when he realized their eyes had met. He shifted a little, folding his arms over his chest, his jaw tightening resolutely. And then the truth struck her.

This wasn't indifference. This was irritation. Anger. But since he had no reason to be angry with her, where was it directed?

For a long, shaky moment she thought about that, until she finally made a decision. She hadn't come here tonight to have him dismiss her so easily. Until she found out what was really going on, she had no intention of leaving.

She took a few steps into the living room. "So you don't want me here. Is that right?"

He continued to stare at the TV. "That's right."

"Well, you showed up at the hotel tonight when I didn't want *you* there. And I wasn't real crazy about running into you in that penthouse, either." She walked into the living room and sat on the sofa. "So I guess now it's your turn to deal with it."

She could tell he was trying to maintain that air of indifference, but she didn't miss the annoyance that bubbled just beneath the surface. Sitting up suddenly, he flipped the TV off and headed to the kitchen. She heard a cabinet door opening and closing, then the grinding of the ice dispenser in the refrigerator door. She walked to the bar that separated the dining room from the kitchen and saw him pour a healthy amount of Scotch into an ice-filled glass.

She rested her forearms casually on the bar. "Why did you leave so suddenly tonight?"

"I told you. I had to make a phone call."

"You didn't make a phone call."

He took a long drink from the glass, then turned and stared at her evenly. "You're right. I didn't make a phone call. It was just time to go."

"I seem to remember you left right after my father asked you what you did for a living."

His expression remained steady, but he was gripping the glass so tightly his knuckles whitened. "I don't like questions like that."

"So what if you get a few questions? You must have at least a dozen good answers for anything my parents could have asked you."

"I do. But after a while…"

"It's hard for you to lie?"

"It's never been hard for me to lie."

"Then what was the problem?"

"Did you *want* me to lie to your parents?"

"Maybe you should consider telling the truth."

"You know I can't do that. My job depends on my anonymity. I have to be careful what I tell people about myself. My life is a puzzle that has to stay in pieces so nobody gets the full picture about who I am."

"Even me?"

"Even you."

"I think this is about more than just your job."

"What do you mean?"

"I don't think you have to be all that secretive about yourself. I think your job is just a convenient excuse to avoid getting too close to anyone."

"What the hell makes you say that?"

"It's the truth, isn't it?"

"No!"

"Sure it is. You wouldn't be angry if it weren't."

His lips tightened. "I don't need your amateur psychoanalysis."

"I'll ask you one more time. Why did you walk out tonight?"

"Because I didn't want to lie!"

"Why not?"

"Because I…" He let out a harsh breath. "Because I care what your parents think of me."

"Why?"

"Will you just drop it?"

"No. I'm not dropping anything. I want to know."

An Important Message
from the Editors

Dear Reader,

If you'd enjoy reading romance novels with larger print that's easier on your eyes, let us send you TWO FREE HARLEQUIN INTRIGUE® NOVELS in our NEW LARGER-PRINT EDITION. These books are complete and unabridged, but the type is set about 25% bigger to make it easier to read. Look inside for an actual-size sample.

By the way, you'll also get a surprise gift with your two free books!

Pam Powers

eel off Seal and
Place Inside...

THE RIGHT WOMAN

she'd thought she was fine. It took Daniel's words and Brooke's question to make her realize she was far from a full recovery.

She'd made a start with her sister's help and she intended to go forward now. Sarah felt as if she'd been living in a darkened room and some-one had suddenly opened a door, letting in the fresh air and sunshine. She could feel its warmth slowly seeping into the coldest part of her. The feeling was liberating. She realized it was only a small step and she had a long way to go, but she was ready to face life again with Serena and her family behind her.

All too soon, they were saying goodbye and Sarah experienced a moment of sadness for all the years she and Serena had missed. But they had each other now and that's what

She held

YOURS FREE!

You'll get a great mystery gift with your two free larger-print books!

GET TWO FREE LARGER-PRINT BOOKS!

YES! Please send me two free Harlequin Intrigue® romantic suspense novels in the larger-print edition, and my free mystery gift, too. I understand that I am under no obligation to purchase anything, as explained on the back of this insert.

199 HDL D7U7   399 HDL D7U9

FIRST NAME	LAST NAME

ADDRESS

APT.#	CITY

STATE/PROV.	ZIP/POSTAL CODE

Are you a current Harlequin Intrigue® subscriber and wa
to receive the larger-print edition?

Call 1-800-221-5011 today!

▼ DETACH AND MAIL CARD TODAY! ▼

(H-ILPP-05/05) © 2004 Harlequin Enterprises Ltd.

The Harlequin Reader Service™ — Here's How It Works:

Accepting your 2 free Harlequin Intrigue® larger-print books and gift places you under no obligation to buy anything. You may keep the books and gift and return the shipping statement marked "cancel." If you do not cancel, about a month later we'll send you 6 additional Harlequin Intrigue larger-print books and bill you just $4.49 each in the U.S., or $5.24 each in Canada, plus 25¢ shipping & handling per book and applicable taxes if any.* That's the complete price and — compared to cover prices of $5.24 each in the U.S. and $6.24 each in Canada — it's quite a bargain! You may cancel at any time, but if you choose to continue, every month we'll send you 6 more books, which you may either purchase at the discount price or return to us and cancel your subscription.

*Terms and prices subject to change without notice. Sales tax applicable in N.Y. Canadian residents will be charged applicable provincial taxes and GST.

"Alyssa—"

"Damn it, I want an explanation! Why does it matter what my parents think of you?"

He slammed his drink down on the counter. "Because of the way I feel about their daughter!"

For a moment Alyssa stopped breathing. *What* did he say?

Derek picked up the glass, started to take another drink, then tossed the contents into the sink with a slosh and a clatter. He set the glass down and started to walk out of the kitchen, but when Alyssa came around and met him at the doorway, he turned away and put his palms on the counter, his shoulders heaving with harsh breaths.

"I don't know why I said that," he told her. "It just came out. It doesn't mean a damned thing."

She stepped into the kitchen. "It doesn't?"

"No. I just…"

"Just what?"

Slowly he straightened and turned around. "You should have left when I told you to. I'll cause you nothing but grief and then I'll walk away. Bank on it."

"I'll take my chances."

"Will you stop being so damned naive?"

"Naiveté has nothing to do with it. I just want to know who you really are."

"You wouldn't like who I really am."

"Why don't you let me be the judge of that?"

She took a step forward and this time it was Derek who stepped back. Stopped by the counter, he took her by the shoulders so she wouldn't come any closer.

"You don't know what you're doing, Lys. I'm not a man you should be messing with."

"I think it's time you made up your mind."

"What?"

"First you give me your address and then you tell me to go away. Then you tell me you have feelings for me, only to hold me at arm's length. Which is it? Do you want me here or don't you?"

"Don't you understand? I don't want to hurt you!"

"The only way you can hurt me is to lie to me. Please don't ever do that again."

For a moment he didn't move. He didn't even breathe. He just stood there, holding her in place. Then his fingers flexed against her, and for a moment she swore he was going to push her away. But instead he came closer, his grip softening to a caress. He stared down at her, his anger and frustration melting into an expression so somber and desolate it sent shivers down her spine. When he spoke, his voice was barely above a whisper.

"In Seattle I got a call," he said. "I had to leave that morning. I had no choice. So I told myself it would be best if I just disappeared. I knew I would miss you, but I had no idea how much. I couldn't lie down to sleep without seeing your face." He paused. "I still can't."

He was describing her experience exactly. She remembered the nights she'd spent lying in bed, feeling hot and restless, trying to get his face out of her mind, trying so hard to forget the man who'd seemed to have forgotten her.

"I know I walked away from you that morning,"

he said, "but please—no matter what I say or do—
please don't walk away from me tonight."

Alyssa was stunned. He spoke quietly, but his
voice was so full of emotion that it almost knocked
her out. She'd had no idea. None at all. No inkling of
just how much he'd missed her and how much he
wanted her here now, no matter how he'd behaved
this evening.

She searched his expression for anything that
might tell her he was manipulating her, stretching the
truth or lying outright, but all she saw was a man
who was as overwhelmed as she was by what was
happening between them.

As they stared at each other, his expression, dark
and haunting in the dim light, slowly shifted into
something more sexual. He touched her cheek, stroking it gently, then leaned in and replaced his fingertips with his lips. After a kiss there, he cradled the
back of her head and dragged his mouth along her
jaw to her neck, where he pressed another kiss, then
another, moving with a slow sensuality that made
her breath come faster and her mouth go dry. She
tilted her head back and closed her eyes as his hot
breath saturated the skin on the side of her neck.
Every move he made felt earnest and sincere, as if he
was silently apologizing for the angry words he'd
spoken.

She still didn't understand this. Understand *him*.
Maybe that would be a long time coming. But now she
knew there was more between them than a week-long
fling and an accidental reunion, that they had some
elemental connection neither of them could deny.

"Tell me you're not going to leave," he said. "Tell me you'll stay with me tonight."

Alyssa's heart jolted at the whispered invitation, desire pooling hot and heavy inside her. There were still so many unanswered questions, and eventually she needed answers to all of them, but now that she'd seen this tiny glimpse inside his heart, those answers could wait.

"Yes," she murmured. "I'll stay."

He skimmed his hands up and down her back in long, restless strokes, then dropped his mouth to the juncture between her neck and shoulder, his lips tugging at the tender skin there.

"I can't believe I'm here," she said, her heartbeat thrumming in her ears. "I told myself not to come, and yet—"

"You can't stay away from me," he said. "Any more than I can stay away from you."

He splayed his hands over the small of her back and pulled her to him, the rigid length of his erection pressing against her, telling her how much he wanted her.

Maybe even as much as she wanted him.

"Come to bed with me," he said.

She had no desire to resist. None at all. She let him take her by the hand and lead her out of the kitchen to his bedroom, which was as barren as the rest of his apartment. It contained nothing but a small dresser and a bed made clumsily with beige sheets and a blanket. The only light in the room came from the streetlamp outside that cast a windowpane shadow on the wall.

Derek gently turned her around, swept her hair

aside and found the zipper of her dress. He lowered it to the small of her back, then shifted the dress off her shoulders, letting it fall into a puddle at her feet. Taking her arm, he helped her step out of it. She tried to turn around, but he stopped her, easing up behind her and reaching around her for the front clasp of her bra. He opened it and swept the cups aside, pressing his palms to her breasts and caressing them in slow circles, his fingers tripping over her nipples. Leaning her head back against his shoulder, she relished the way he was caressing her, with a slow, sweet tenderness that took her breath away.

He pulled her bra off and tossed it to the floor. When she turned around, her gaze was caught by the strip of bare skin revealed by his unbuttoned shirt. Touching her fingertips to his throat, she dragged them down to his breastbone, watching her hand as it descended inch by inch. She flattened her palm against his abdomen, moving it lower still. When her hand tripped over the waistband of his jeans, she hooked her finger into a belt loop and eased him toward her, wrapping her other hand behind his neck and pulling his mouth down to meet hers. As she kissed him, she slipped both hands beneath his shirt and pushed it off his shoulders, and he dropped his arms to let it fall behind him.

She reached for his belt, but he stopped her, instead taking her by the hand and leading her to the bed. He coaxed her to sit, then surprised her by kneeling on the carpet in front of her. Pressing her legs apart, he moved between them, sliding his hands up and down her thighs in a gentle caress, his dark gaze focused on her face.

"No matter what has happened between us," he said, "I swear I never meant to hurt you. Do you believe that?"

All she could do was dip her head in a single nod, so lost in the feeling of his hands on her and sound of his gentle words that she couldn't speak.

"I've had a hard life, Lys," he murmured. "The time we spent in Seattle just might have been the best week I've ever had."

She couldn't imagine what his life had been like, but his unwavering gaze and earnest expression told her that he was stating a painful truth—one that came from a place so deep inside him that dredging it up was a chore.

She rested her palm against his cheek, then leaned forward to meet his mouth in a long, deep kiss. She couldn't count the number of times they'd made love in Seattle, but it had never felt like this.

After a while he pulled away and rested his palms against her shoulders. "Lie back, sweetheart."

As she lay back on the bed, Derek hooked his fingers into her panties. She lifted her hips and he slowly pulled them down, then tossed them aside. She tried to sit up, but he gently pushed her down. When he stroked her thighs again, working his way closer to the soft curls at the apex of her thighs, she let out a soft, blissful sigh as her body tensed with anticipation.

He knelt closer, his fingers finding the soft folds between her legs and touching her hot, swollen flesh. He slid his fingers inside, then pulled back to stroke her again, in and out, back and forth, over and over, with a single-minded intensity that astonished her.

This was what she'd missed so much—his sure hands tending to her in all the right places in all the right ways, knowing, somehow, what she needed the most. And when he finally lowered his mouth to her, she took a deep, shuddering breath and clutched the blanket in tight fists. He used his tongue and his lips in a gentle rhythmic motion and she arched against him, her thighs tightening with expectation and her body screaming for release.

She reached for him. "Derek...I want you with me...*please*..."

He slid away and stood, stepping back to free himself of the rest of his clothes. By the time he'd found a condom and returned to her, she thought she'd go crazy with wanting him. He climbed onto the bed, the mattress dipping with his weight. Then he moved between her parted thighs, dropping a palm to the blanket on either side of her, staring down at her with eyes so dark and passionate that she trembled at the sight. She traced her fingertips over his cheek, his chin, then the fullness of his lower lip.

"It's been such a long time," she whispered.

"Too long," he said.

He slid inside her and she gasped at the sheer pleasure of it. After a few slow, concentrated strokes, he built momentum, until he was thrusting hard and deep. She curled her legs around him, clutching his shoulders, asking for more, and he gave her everything she wanted with the kind of breathtaking intensity that made the room spin around her. She was lost in the feeling, drowning in it, struggling to drag air into her lungs. She didn't know if he understood she was right there with him on the way to release, or whether he was so lost in his own need that he couldn't slow down even if he wanted to. This was it. This was the kind of raw, wild, demanding sex that she'd only dreamed about until she'd met Derek. She felt as if she was totally at his mercy, as if she'd lost all sense of autonomy, as if they weren't two people, but one. She was so suffused with sensation, so racked by desire, that her climax came in a matter of seconds. She cried out with pleasure, feeling every shattering moment all the way to her soul.

"Oh, Lys, oh, *damn...*"

Derek's body went rigid. He dropped his head to her shoulder, letting out a deep, rasping groan that seemed to shudder through his whole body. He held her tightly, rocking against her as the waves of pleasure rolled through both of them. After several long, harsh breaths, he collapsed over her, his breath hot against her neck. Alyssa ran her hands up and down his back, lost in his scent, in his warmth, in the very idea that she was with him like this when she'd thought she'd never see him again.

Finally he fell away and rolled onto his back, reaching out blindly until he found her hand. He held it tightly, clinging to her as if she might get up and leave him at any moment.

Please don't walk away from me tonight.

Derek was a maddening mass of contradictions that Alyssa didn't know if she'd ever figure out. The answer was inside him somewhere, though. She only hoped he'd let her close enough to find out what it was.

10

DEREK AND ALYSSA lay in silence for several minutes, neither of them saying a word. He had no idea what to think. None at all. He'd tried his damnedest to warn her, to drive her out the door, because as much as he wanted her here tonight, he'd told her the truth. In the end, he'd only cause her grief.

But she'd stayed. And he had no clue where they went from here.

Don't think about that now. Just think about her.

He turned over onto his side, bunching the pillow beneath his head, still holding her hand. Alyssa took a deep, cleansing breath, her body melting into total relaxation.

She turned to face him. "You were right before."

"About what?"

"When I was on that stage tonight and looked up to see you there, in spite of everything…"

"Yes?"

"I was glad to see you."

He'd been stabbing in the dark when he'd said that. Challenging her. Trying something—anything—to keep her from sending him away. And now he knew. Even when she'd protested later, in those first few seconds when he'd shown up, her last thought had been to ask him to leave.

"You looked beautiful," he told her. "I don't think I ever got around to telling you that."

"You looked pretty nice yourself. I'd never seen you in a suit before."

"Tomorrow it's going to be a tuxedo."

"A tux? Why?"

"A former member of my team is getting married at noon. I'm his best man."

She looked at him strangely.

"What?" he asked.

"A wedding. It just seems so...I don't know. *Ordinary*."

"So what am I? Extraordinary?"

She sighed contentedly. "Oh, yeah."

As she spoke, he was reminded of how her voice sounded after they made love, floating across the darkness on waves of total satisfaction, a voice he could lie here and listen to for the rest of his life.

"Actually," she said, "I was thinking about the fact that you're not exactly a run-of-the-mill kind of guy. Look at what you were doing in that penthouse."

"It's ordinary for me."

She smiled. "Yeah. I guess it is." She rolled onto her side so she was face-to-face with him. "So the groom is a former member of your team? What is he doing now?"

"He has a security firm. He contracts everything from on-site armed security to bodyguard services. He has some out-of-town clients, but for the most part his business keeps him in Dallas."

"So he lives here, too?"

"Yeah. And with luck, he'll actually make it back here for his wedding."

"What do you mean?"

"He's in Washington. My regular pilot was out sick, so I asked Gus to do one last job for me. He's the one who flew Gerald Owens to Washington for interrogation."

"And he might not make it back?"

"He was held up getting to Washington because of bad weather there. He's flying back in the morning. As long as nothing else goes wrong, he'll make it."

"So Owens is being interrogated? What do you hope to find out from him?"

Derek hesitated, even as he was beginning to realize that what Alyssa had said earlier held more truth than he cared to admit. He'd always told himself that secrecy was absolutely essential to what he did, and in most cases, it was. But a lot of the time, his secrecy stemmed more from his distrust of people in general than it did from the need to keep everything about his work confidential.

Alyssa already knew the essence of what was happening with Owens, and whether Derek trusted her with more information was his call. And he knew that after all the lies he'd told her, the more truth he could reveal, the closer he'd come to repairing the damage he'd done.

"Owens is just a gun for hire collecting the blackmail material for somebody else," he told her. "We don't know that person's identity. All we know is that he wants to influence the outcome of a vote on a trade bill coming before the House of Representatives on Monday morning."

"You're kidding."

"Wish I were."

"So that's the kind of thing you deal with?"

"That's the least of what I deal with."

"Monday morning. That doesn't give you much time."

"With luck, Owens will crack and tell us who hired him and where the other DVDs are. That's when I'll swing back into action and retrieve them. That call could come in five minutes, tomorrow, the next day, or never. I have no way of knowing."

"With Gus stuck in Washington on the eve of his wedding, I bet his fiancée is going crazy."

"I smoothed things over with her tonight at the rehearsal dinner. Gus has always known I'd take a bullet for him. Never thought it would come to that but, believe me, I took one right between the eyes tonight."

Alyssa smiled. "So that was where you were before you showed up at the hotel?"

"Yes."

He slid his arm around her and she scooted over and laid her head on his shoulder, resting her palm against his chest. She draped her thigh casually over his and he stroked it gently.

"Your apartment," she said. "It's not what I expected."

"I'm afraid I don't have much decorating sense."

"Is that why it's so…"

"Barren?"

"Exactly."

He laughed a little. "Yeah, that's part of it. The other part is that..." He glanced around. "It's just me here, and not that often. Doesn't seem to be much point in bothering to make it look like home."

"But it is your home."

"I guess it's the closest thing I've got to one."

"Do you have family in Dallas?"

"No."

"Where do they live?"

"It doesn't matter."

She frowned. "It's not that personal a question, is it?"

"No. It's not. And I'm not being evasive." He paused again. "Actually, I don't have one."

Alyssa pulled back, sure she couldn't have heard him right. "You don't have a family?"

"I was raised by my uncle. And he's dead now."

"Your uncle?"

"Yeah. My mother wasn't exactly competent. And who knew where the hell my father was? Or, for that matter, *who* he was."

Alyssa couldn't believe this. She'd had no idea Derek had a background like that. Now that she remembered, when they were in Seattle, talking about his past was another of the things he'd sidestepped before turning the focus of the conversation back to her.

"So you never even knew your own father?" she asked.

"No."

"And your mother was unfit to raise a child?"

"Yeah. Alcohol and drugs will do that to a person."

He spoke nonchalantly, as if he was relating somebody else's story.

"How old were you when you went to live with your uncle?"

"I was ten."

Alyssa was stunned. Ten years old, and his mother had essentially abandoned him?

"Was it okay living with your uncle?"

Derek shrugged. "Yeah. It was fine. He fed me, put clothes on my back. But he ran a business, a bar. He was gone when I got home from school and he didn't get back until three in the morning. I saw him on the weekends."

"He left a ten-year-old boy home alone every night?"

"He was a single man saddled with a kid he hadn't asked for. He did the best he could. It kept me from going into the foster care system. And anything beat what I'd had with my mother. It was better to have no parent at all than one who was as messed up as she was."

He spoke carelessly, almost flippantly, but she sensed a vulnerability beneath his facade of indifference. No child could go through something like that without it having a profound effect on him.

"I'm betting you never came home to an empty house in your life," he said.

"Not when I was that age."

He shifted a little, his face falling into a frown.

"What?"

"Nothing."

"No, tell me."

He laughed a little, but it sounded hollow. "I remember sitting in my uncle's apartment in the afternoons watching those old sitcoms on TV. And I used to think about what it would be like to be one of those kids, with a mom who stayed home and baked cookies and tucked you in at night and a dad who dispensed all that wisdom, even when you screwed up. And you knew at the end of that half hour, no matter how many problems came up, everything was going to be okay again. I used to imagine that was the kind of life I had."

As she pictured him sitting and watching those shows, wishing he could have that kind of family, she felt a tightness in her throat as if she were going to cry.

"Nobody really has that kind of childhood," she said.

"You came close."

He was right. Her childhood hadn't been the pinnacle of perfection those old TV shows were, but at its heart it was the same. She'd been raised in a loving, supportive family.

Derek clearly hadn't.

"You said your uncle died. When was that?"

"A few months after my eighteenth birthday. He tried to break up a fight in his bar. He was shot and killed."

"God, Derek. That's terrible. I'm so sorry."

"To tell you the truth, I really didn't know him all that well. Yeah, I suppose I was sad when he was gone, but…"

"What?"

"I don't know. It was as if an acquaintance had died, or a neighbor or something. It was as if we weren't even related."

He spoke softly, with little emotion, but that was what made his words seem so bleak. Alyssa couldn't imagine such a thing. Her heart broke for the boy he must have been and the isolation he must have felt.

"What did you do then?" she asked.

"I didn't have a lot of options. College was out of the question for a kid like me. I'd barely graduated high school. So I went into the military. It offered me three meals a day, a place to live and the chance to make something of myself."

"Smart move."

"It wasn't easy, though. See, I had a small problem with authority. I wasn't used to somebody telling me what to do."

And she knew why. Because he'd essentially been on his own all his life and had answered to no one.

"But that's how I eventually ended up doing what I'm doing now," Derek said. "I might work for the government, but I do it on a contract basis only. I decide what jobs I take and nobody questions how I get them done. They just want results. And they're willing to pay me quite well to get them."

"So it's a lucrative business."

"Let's just say I live beneath my means."

"In other words, *very* lucrative."

"And it's amazing what a good financial planner can do. I pretty much just hand him the money and get out of his way."

"So is having a lot of money important to you?"

He thought about that for a moment. "No, not really."

"You have no family to share it with."

"That's why I can make the money. Because I don't have family ties. I can pick up and go anywhere I need to whenever I need to. It's actually an asset in my line of work."

"Maybe that's good for your job," she said. "But what is it like when you come home again?"

"Like I said, I'm not here very often."

"Do you ever wish you had a life that was a little more permanent?"

"I don't think about that."

He spoke offhandedly, but she heard a note of tension in his voice. He was lying. But it wasn't a lie he told to deceive her. It was a lie he told to deceive himself.

"Where is your mother now?"

"I have no idea."

"She's still your family. Sometimes people change—"

"No. She'll never change."

"Maybe someday—"

"No. I have no desire ever to see her again. Coming from where you do, I know it's hard for you to understand that. But this isn't one of those situations where a TV psychologist can take an hour and patch up a relationship. I've written off that part of my life."

Alyssa sighed. "I don't blame you for that. It's just such a sad thing."

"I warned you that you might not like the man I really am."

"You mean, the man who pulled himself up out of bad circumstances and made something of himself? Actually, I admire him a lot."

They lay there in silence for a long time, Alyssa curled in Derek's arms, her head against his chest, the steady beating of his heart lulling her toward sleep. She meant every word of what she'd said. She did admire him for what he'd accomplished, especially given where he'd come from. But she wondered, too, about the personal toll he'd suffered to get there.

"Derek?" she said.

"Uh-huh?"

"Your uncle."

"What about him?"

"Did he love you?"

Derek opened his eyes and looked down at her. "What?"

"I said, did he love you?"

He turned away again, staring into the darkness. Suddenly he seemed lost, like a man who knew there was something in life he was missing, but he just couldn't grasp it.

"I don't know," he whispered.

And then she did cry, silent tears falling from her eyes. She wiped them away with her fingertips, then wrapped her arm around him. She couldn't fathom what it must have been like for him as a child, lying in bed at night in a dark, empty house, knowing there wasn't a soul on the planet who loved him. She didn't know how anyone could raise a child, no matter what the circumstances, without giving him something to hold on to, some kind of anchor, some kind of emotional sustenance.

She was a capable woman because she'd had the support of a loving family. Derek was a capable man because he'd learned early to deal with the kinds of things no child should ever have to face.

She'd thought it was the facts of his life that she wanted to know—names, places, dates. But the things he'd revealed to her tonight told her so much more than that. She knew now why he lived a life that didn't allow him to connect with anyone.

Because it was all he'd ever known.

THE NEXT MORNING, Alyssa woke slowly, a little disoriented at first. Several seconds passed before it all came back to her—where she was, what she'd done.

And who she'd done it with.

The moment Derek's face came to mind, she rolled over and reached for him.

He wasn't there.

She glanced at the clock. It was five minutes after five.

She threw back the covers and rose to sit on the edge of the bed for a moment, trying to get her bearings. By the faint light of the streetlamp filtering through the window, she saw her dress lying in a heap on the floor and Derek's shirt crumpled beside it.

Where was he?

She had a sudden flashback to that morning in Seattle when he'd left her before she'd woken, then told herself that was silly. This was his apartment. He couldn't have just disappeared.

She grabbed his shirt and put it on, then walked quietly down the hall, catching the scent of coffee brewing. Peering around the doorway, she was relieved to see Derek sitting at the kitchen table, his back to her. He wore only a pair of jeans. A cup of coffee sat in front of him. His elbows were on the table and his chin rested on his fists. For a long time he just sat there, staring straight ahead, and she sensed that something wasn't right. Then he let out a heavy sigh and dropped his head to his hands.

As the truth of the situation struck her, the relief she'd felt at seeing him turned to apprehension. He'd awakened this morning and regretted that he'd given her his address. Regretted that he'd opened up to her the way he had. Now he wished she wasn't here and he didn't know what to do about it. The sight of him caught in such a dilemma wiped away every bit of the euphoria she'd felt last night.

Fighting the sinking feeling in her stomach, she walked into the kitchen. He looked up.

"Lys. You're awake."

"Yeah. I wondered where you were."

He reached over and pulled out a chair. "Sit down. I need to tell you something."

The tone of his voice said something bad was coming and she was afraid she knew what it was. She lowered herself to the chair, her heart beating like crazy. But still she had enough wits about her to speak first before he told her what she didn't want to hear.

"Look, Derek. I'll make this easy for you, okay? Just because I know where you live now, just because we were together last night, it doesn't mean I'm presuming anything about the two of us."

"What?"

"You think you made a mistake last night and now you want out again. Isn't that right?"

He looked at her with surprise. "What are you talking about?"

"I can tell by the look on your face. You're clearly getting ready to tell me something I don't want to hear."

"Yes, that's true. But it has nothing to do with us."

"What, then?"

Derek took her hands in his. "Do you remember I told you that Owens was only the middle man? That he was working for someone else?"

"Yes."

"I just had a phone call. Owens talked. We know now who ordered the blackmail."

"Who is it?"

"His name is Lawrence Teague."

11

"LAWRENCE TEAGUE?" Alyssa said. "My boss?"

"Yes."

She stared dumbly at Derek. "But that can't be."

"It is."

Alyssa sat there, speechless, as the thought sank in. The hood lamp over the stove was the only light Derek had turned on, and with the early hour and her head throbbing dully from lack of sleep and the coffeepot gurgling and hissing, the atmosphere seemed almost surreal. And now this revelation...

"I just can't imagine him doing this. Why is he blackmailing congressmen? What could he hope to gain?"

"Real estate isn't all he has going. Apparently he's heavily invested in manufacturing in the Far East. If the trade bill that's coming to the House floor on Monday morning passes, he could be out millions."

Alyssa felt as if the ground had fallen away beneath her feet. "I've worked for him for over four years. He just doesn't seem like the kind of man who would do something like that."

"Some men do desperate things for money."

"But blackmail congressmen?"

"My contact in Washington tells me that Owens spilled everything. They doubt he's lying."

"Has Teague done this before?"

"Not to our knowledge. But if you have enough money and you want a job done, it's not hard to find someone to do it."

"And the guy available to do it just happened to be living in one of his buildings?"

"No. It was the other way around. Apparently in order to entice Owens to take this job, Teague offered him a year lease on the penthouse apartment at the Waterford."

Alyssa couldn't believe this. All this had been going on right under her nose?

Lawrence Teague had been like an icon to her, a man whose success and business expertise had always inspired her. To discover that he was a criminal was incomprehensible to her.

"I need a cup of coffee," she said, rising from her chair. "Cups?"

"Cabinet to the left of the stove."

She poured some coffee, then turned around and leaned against the counter. "So what happens now?"

"Owens is sure Teague is holding the DVDs in his apartment in the Houston building."

"The Concorde?"

"Yes. I need to get them. My contact wants to make sure the incriminating evidence is destroyed before Monday morning."

"How do you plan to do that?"

"We found out that Teague is flying into Dallas this morning. My team will grab him. On the way to

Houston, I'll interrogate him to make sure Owens was telling the truth. Then I'll break into the penthouse and get the DVDs. Since there's no housekeeping service on Saturdays, and since he lives alone, it's unlikely I'll run into anyone."

"You make it sound so easy."

"Sweetheart, nothing I do is easy."

"Well, this one may be harder than you think."

"Why?"

"Have you checked out the security system at the Concorde?"

"Not yet."

"It's state-of-the-art."

"Yeah. So is the Waterford's system. Sorry to burst your bubble, but getting through those highly integrated systems is a piece of cake."

"Not when they use biometrics."

Derek's face fell. "Oh, crap. What kind?"

"Retinal scanners. On all the perimeter doors. If your retina isn't scanned into the system, you can't get inside."

"That seems like overkill for an apartment building."

"Teague thinks the more state-of-the-art his security systems are, the more likely he is to attract wealthy, high-profile tenants. Eventually he plans to install them in all his buildings."

Derek blew out a breath. "Damn. Breaching a retinal scanner is next to impossible." He thought for a moment, then shook his head. "My only other alternative is to take Teague inside with me to get the DVDs, but he'd essentially be a hostage in a public situation. That's a scenario that's hard to control."

"There's a way around it."

"How's that?"

"Take me instead."

"What?"

"I'm at the managerial level with Starlight, which means I have access to all their buildings."

"Your retinas have been scanned into the system?"

"Yes. They did it when I went to the grand opening of the Concorde a few months ago. But I can only get you through the perimeter doors. I can't get you up the elevator to the penthouse."

"Not a problem. Teague will be carrying his key card. I'm sure I can persuade him to let us borrow it."

She nodded in agreement. "Have you given any thought to how you plan to grab Teague?"

"My men will have to play that by ear."

"Maybe not. I'm picking him up at the airport."

Derek stared at her for a moment, and she could see his wheels turning. "Had you planned on using your own car?"

"No, I have a limousine reserved. Teague expects that kind of treatment."

"Perfect," Derek said. "That limousine is going to take a little detour on its way to the Waterford, straight to where our jet is hangared."

"Teague will obviously object to that. How are you going to get the driver to do it?"

"That's not a problem, as long as I'm the driver."

Alyssa smiled. "Good plan."

"You're making things easy for me."

"Are you sure the people you work for won't have any problem with you recruiting an amateur to help?"

"My team operates independently. I have total authority to use any method necessary to get the job done."

"Wait a minute," Alyssa said. "How are we getting to Houston?"

"That's the only hang-up. We can't fly commercial because we have to bring Teague along in case we hit a snag and it becomes necessary to take him into the apartment building with us. And we need to get this job done ASAP, because if it turns out that Owens is lying, we'll need time to reevaluate the situation before Monday morning. Gus is my only option."

"Gus? You're going to ask him to fly us to Houston? On his wedding day?"

"I already have."

"And what did he say?"

"I've got a pretty extensive vocabulary of four-letter words, but he used a few even I hadn't heard."

"But he's going to do it?"

"Yeah. He's going to do it."

"Even if you two might not make it back for the wedding?"

"We'll make it. Gus should be touching down just before we need to take off. A quick refueling and he can get the plane in the air again."

"But the wedding's at noon. You're telling me we're going to fly to Houston and back before then?"

Derek checked his watch. "It's five twenty-five now. Teague's flight comes in at Love Field at five after seven. With your help, we'll be able to grab him, get him on the plane and be in the air by seven-thirty. The flight to Houston is only about forty-five minutes, with a fifteen-minute drive from the airport to the Concorde. If all goes well, we can get the job done and be back in the air by nine-thirty, in Dallas by ten-thirty, and to the hotel by eleven."

Alyssa gave him a dumbfounded stare. "So it's as easy as that."

"As I said before, nothing I do is easy."

"This is crazy."

"Nope. Just another day at the office."

"For you, maybe."

Derek's expression grew solemn. "This is a routine job, and you've made it even easier for me. But I should warn you, Alyssa. There's always an element of danger, no matter how well planned the operation is. Are you sure you want to help?"

"Yes. Of course."

He continued to stare at her. "I still don't know if this is a good idea."

"You already said that taking Teague in with you is dangerous. If you take me, we can walk right through the door and nobody will have a clue what's happening. Do you really expect anything to go wrong?"

"No, but—"

"Then it's settled. I'm going with you."

Derek finally nodded reluctantly.

"And I don't care how dangerous it is. If it'll take Teague down, I'm in. Any man who would try to blackmail congressmen deserves to go to jail."

"No. He won't be arrested."

"What?"

"We just need to get the DVDs."

"Wait a minute. He blackmails U.S. congressmen and he walks *away?*"

"If he's arrested and tried, the blackmail material will be brought out in court. What those congressmen don't want the world to know—the content of those DVDs—will be a matter of public record."

"I'm not seeing how justice is being served here."

"It's not. But that's the way it is. It's more important to protect the reputations of the congressmen than it is to prosecute a blackmailer. On Monday morning, Teague will be back to business as usual."

"And what happens if he decides to blackmail more congressmen in the future?"

"From now on, the government will be watching him. He won't dare step outside the law again."

Alyssa took a sip of coffee, thinking about the utter and complete unfairness of it. But she realized now that in the world Derek worked in, nothing was black and white.

"Alyssa?"

She looked up. "Yes?"

Derek rose from his chair and moved to where she stood. "When you first came into the kitchen this morning, did you really think I was going to tell you I'd made a mistake last night? That I didn't want to see you anymore?"

She looked away. "Yes."

He sighed. "Well, I guess I can't blame you for that, can I?"

Derek took her coffee cup from her hand and set

it on the counter, then pulled her into his arms. But in spite of his reassurances, she felt a twinge of apprehension. She wondered how long it would be before she could shake the feeling that he was always just moments away from slipping out of sight, never to be seen again.

DEREK TOLD ALYSSA to cancel the limousine she had coming, then sent her home so she could take a quick shower and change clothes. He did the same at his apartment, putting on a suit again so he could play the part of a limousine driver. He made a phone call, and an hour later he was driving a limousine into the covered entrance of the Waterford and parking at the curb to wait for Alyssa.

His body felt tingly from lack of sleep and he took a sip of coffee from the travel mug he'd brought with him. He'd turned the radio on low to a classic-rock station, hoping the music would help keep him alert. There had been a time when he could subsist on three hours of sleep, a pot of coffee and adrenaline.

Those days were gone.

He'd phoned Kevin to tell him that he wouldn't be needing him after all. Then he'd called Gus back on a secure ground-to-air connection so he could fill him in on the plan he'd put together. Then he'd told him that Alyssa would be helping them out.

Derek knew Gus had been astonished at the mention of Alyssa's name, and now that she was involved to this degree, he'd had to come clean about how he'd run into her yesterday in the penthouse at the Waterford. Gus was the only person who knew about the week they'd spent together in Seattle. And being Gus, he didn't think twice about prying.

Oh, yeah? Alyssa, huh? Imagine meeting up with her again. So...how's that going?

Derek had told him he needed to keep his mind on flying the plane instead of on his friend's love life. Even so, Derek knew Gus only wanted him to be as happy as he was right now, to follow in his matrimonial footsteps and settle down. But Gus just didn't understand that they were different men with different lives and chances were that they'd keep heading down different paths. Still, as difficult as the concept of settling down was for Derek, he couldn't say he hadn't thought about it.

With a heavy sigh, he leaned his head against the headrest, thoughts of last night drifting through his mind. He thought about how Alyssa had stayed with him in spite of the way he'd treated her. Thank God, she gave everyone the benefit of the doubt, including him. He wondered, though, how many more times she'd be so benevolent before she got sick and tired of him and moved on.

She'd told him she admired him for making his way through the quagmire of his childhood. But she didn't have a clue what was really going on inside him. How he might look strong and capable on the outside, but inside...*God*. She had no idea just how screwed up he really was. That the very idea of having to hold up his end of a relationship was frightening at best, inconceivable at worst. But that didn't make him want her any less. It just made her seem like a pipe dream he could never have.

Your uncle…did he love you?

The moment Alyssa had asked that question, his mind had overflowed with dark images of what his life had been like back then. The stark loneliness he'd felt. The fear of abandonment. The aching sense of having no one in the world to depend on but himself.

He couldn't believe he'd told her all that. It had made him feel weak and powerless, and never in his life had he been able to afford to feel like that even for a moment. But then he'd heard the catch in her voice. Felt her tears on his chest. Suddenly it was as if a small part of the pain he'd experienced in his life had faded away, and he knew why. Because Alyssa was feeling it for him. In that moment he'd known with absolute certainty that, at least last night, he'd done the right thing by begging her to stay.

Movement caught the corner of his eye and he turned to see the glass doors swing open and Alyssa come out of the building. She wore a tailored blouse and a pair of pants, looking sharp and professional, ready to make Teague believe that she was merely there to escort him from the airport to the Waterford.

Teague was in for one hell of a surprise.

Derek stepped out of the driver's seat, circled the limo, and opened the back door for her.

"Good morning, madam," he said.

"Good morning," she said brightly, then spoke under her breath. "Sure I can't ride up front with the driver?"

"Oh, no, madam," he whispered back. "That wouldn't be appropriate. I'm just the hired help."

He gave her a smile and closed the door, then circled back to the driver's door and got into the car. He started it and pulled away from the building.

He glanced at his watch. "I phoned the airline. Teague's flight is on time. We should be there with a few minutes to spare."

"Sorry I was a little late getting downstairs," she said. "One of my tenants cornered me."

"This is Saturday. Do they ever let you rest?"

"She just needed to talk to me."

"Big problem?"

"Not really. She just wanted to know if I'd take her dog to the vet next week."

"I didn't know pet transportation was part of your job description."

"Not usually. But her dog is having some health problems and she's a little phobic about doctors' offices."

"Even a veterinarian's office?"

"She lost her husband a few months ago. She doesn't have family close by, so that dog's about all she has. I think she's afraid if she goes to the vet, she's going to hear more bad news."

"If there's bad news, she'll have to hear it sooner or later."

"Yeah, but it's better coming from me. She's been through a lot lately. If it makes her life easier and it's no big deal for me, why not?"

Why not?

That was a good question. Until he'd met Alyssa, he could have stated a dozen reasons why not and believed every one of them. But she never would have believed them. In every aspect of her life, she led with her heart. With anyone else, he might have dismissed that as illogical or impractical or even downright dangerous. But when he saw it in her, it drew him to her in a way he never could have imagined.

"How did you manage to get a limousine on such short notice?" Alyssa asked.

"Money talks, and I've got a big budget."

"I guess so. This is nice."

"Nothing's too good for the big boss."

"I still can't believe he's blackmailing congressmen. He's a multimillionaire. He has everything a man could want. Why would he do this?"

"Because of what we talked about earlier. He stands to lose quite a bit of that money."

"But is it worth ruining six men's lives to keep that from happening?"

"There are plenty of people in this world who would answer yes to that question."

She shook her head. "I still can't believe it."

Derek knew that was true. She couldn't believe it. She was the kind of person who expected the best from people and was astonished when they didn't live up to it. Derek, on the other hand, had no expectations. In his line of work, he'd seen enough corrupt people to last him a lifetime, and they came in all shapes and sizes. That a respected businessman like Teague was engaging in criminal behavior wasn't the least bit surprising to him.

"I can't believe you talked Gus into flying us to Houston," Alyssa said. "What did he tell his fiancée?"

"That he'll be at the church by eleven-fifteen."

"And what if something goes wrong?"

"Nothing's going to go wrong. I value my life too much for that."

"Yes. You told me things could get dangerous."

"It's not the job I'm sweating. It's Gus. If I don't get him to his wedding on time, I'm a dead man."

Alyssa smiled. "He must be a really good friend."

"Uh-huh. A man with murder on his mind, and I'm his target."

"No. A man who sacrifices himself to help you out in a crisis. You'd do the same thing for him, wouldn't you?"

"Like I said. Gus and I go way back."

A plane passed close overhead, which meant they were only a few miles from the airport. He checked his watch. Everything was going according to schedule.

"My God," Alyssa said.

Derek snapped to attention, glancing into the rearview mirror. "What?"

"I just thought of something."

"What?"

"When all this is over with, Teague is going free."

"Yeah. We talked about that."

"But that means I'll be working for a criminal."

"It's okay, Lys. No one will know that, and he's certainly not going to tell anyone."

"That doesn't matter. *I'll* know." She sat back in her seat with an expression of disbelief. "I can't continue to work for a man like him. I'll have to quit."

Derek hadn't thought about that. Even with Teague in Houston most of the time, she wouldn't even want to be associated with any company he ran. It wouldn't matter to some people, but he should have known it would matter to Alyssa.

"Don't worry," he told her. "You won't have any trouble finding another job."

"But it's not just my job. It's my apartment, too. And the people at the Waterford. When I finally got this position in Dallas, Teague told me I could stay put, that he wouldn't transfer me anywhere else since my family was here." She shrugged weakly. "I guess I just imagined that I'd be here for a long time, you know?"

"I'm sorry."

"No," she said. "This isn't your fault. You didn't cause the problem. You're just eliminating it."

"But if we hadn't run into each other in that penthouse, you wouldn't have had to know any of this."

"No. I'm better off knowing. I don't want to work for a man like him."

But the catch in her voice told Derek just how heartbroken she was, and suddenly he hated that Alyssa had gotten caught up in this situation, and now she was going to be the one to pay the price for it. The very idea that Teague's greed was forcing her to pull up the roots she'd so lovingly put down was intolerable.

Derek decided he'd have to do something about that.

A few minutes later they pulled up to the terminal at Love Field. He got out of the car and opened Alyssa's door. When she stepped out, he spoke quietly to her.

"Just do what we discussed. Pick Teague up as you would on any other day. Act nonchalant. Make pleasant conversation."

"And once everything starts to go down?"

"Just play dumb. Gus and I will take care of everything."

12

ALYSSA MET Lawrence Teague at baggage claim, not surprised in the least to see the trim fifty-four-year-old man wearing a suit and carrying a briefcase, looking every bit like the excruciatingly serious, organized and methodical man he was. She'd long suspected that he wore the suit to bed and kept his briefcase beside his dresser in the event that a business meeting broke out in his bedroom in the middle of the night. *Success is ninety percent perspiration and ten percent inspiration,* she'd heard him say more than once, and even on the short commuter hop from Houston to Dallas, she had no doubt he'd spent that time with his briefcase open, perspiring. Up to now, she'd admired him for being a self-made millionaire. But now that she knew just what lengths he'd go to to hang on to those millions, that admiration had turned to disgust.

He greeted her with a cursory nod, grabbed his bag from the baggage carousel and they started down the terminal. Alyssa had felt nervous enough while she was waiting for Teague. Now that he was here and they were heading toward the limousine, that nervousness took a quantum leap.

It's okay. Derek knows what he's doing.

"How is the weather here today?" Teague asked.

"Sunny and seventy-two," she replied.

"It was already eighty-four degrees in Houston when I left. Love the city. Detest the weather."

"Unfortunately," Alyssa said, "the high in Dallas today is in the nineties. I'm afraid you can't escape the Texas heat."

He sighed. "It's too hot in Texas, too rainy in Seattle, too cold in New York. I swear I'm constructing my next building in the Hawaiian Islands. And I'll be its first tenant."

She smiled obligingly, hoping it didn't look as phony as it felt.

"So," he said, "how are things at the Waterford?"

For a moment Alyssa thought she heard suspicion in his voice. Had he heard about the broken window in the penthouse? Until now she hadn't considered that he might have, but she supposed it was possible. If he'd also heard that the police had investigated because some of the tenants thought they'd heard a gunshot, he could get suspicious that it had something to do with Owens.

"Things are running smoothly," she told him.

"Good. I expected as much."

She watched him out of the corner of her eye as they walked and, after a few moments, she decided she'd only been imagining the warm tone in his voice. He hadn't heard a thing about the window. And she was going to have to stop suspecting him of being suspicious or she was going to look suspicious herself.

When they exited the terminal, Alyssa saw Derek standing next to the limousine. With just the right amount of deference, he approached them and took Teague's bag. He opened the rear door for them and they got inside. He put the bag in the trunk, then slid behind the wheel. Alyssa told him they wanted to go to the Waterford, gave him the cross streets, as she would any driver, then settled back in the seat. Derek started the engine and pulled away from the curb.

"Congratulations on the award you received from your alma mater," Teague said. "The ceremony was last night, wasn't it?"

"Yes, sir."

"Very impressive. You've been doing a wonderful job at the Waterford, just as you did at the Seattle property. Tenant satisfaction has never been this high. Don't think your efforts have gone unnoticed."

"Thank you, sir," she said, hoping her voice didn't reflect that his opinion had become completely irrelevant to her. "I've enjoyed every moment of the job."

Then Teague got a confused look on his face. "Excuse me, but where is the driver going?"

"I don't know." Alyssa leaned forward. "Sir, I believe you're going the wrong direction."

"It's a detour, ma'am. There's road construction on Mockingbird Lane."

Alyssa settled back in her seat. "Road construction," she repeated.

She continued to make small talk with Teague, her nervousness increasing when Derek took a left turn back onto airport property. For a while, Teague didn't seem to notice. Then he sat up suddenly and glanced out the window.

"Where are we going?" He leaned forward and tapped on the seat in front of him. "Driver, you're going the wrong way."

Derek made a hard right. He pulled through an open gate and drove across an expanse of blacktop past several private planes. Ahead was a large metal building she assumed was a hangar. The door of the building slid open.

"Hey!" Teague shouted. "What the hell do you think you're doing?"

Alyssa looked appropriately fearful, just as Derek had instructed her to, as if she didn't have a clue what was going on. Actually, it wasn't too hard to look fearful, considering the fact that her heart was hammering in her chest and she was gripping the seat so tightly in anticipation of what was coming she was practically clawing through it.

Derek drove into the hangar and Alyssa heard the metal door slam closed behind them. Before he'd even brought the car to a halt, Teague's door flew open and he was looking down the barrel of a gun.

"Out of the car!" the man holding the gun said. "*Move!*"

His eyes wide with apprehension, Teague did as he was told. The man grabbed him by the arm, spun him around and shoved him against the fender. Derek was already out of the driver's seat and in an instant he had Teague in handcuffs.

"What the hell is going on here?" Teague demanded. Derek said nothing. The man with the gun led

Teague toward the jet and hustled him aboard. Alyssa put her hand against her chest, wondering if the events of the past few moments could induce a heart attack.

Derek came around and opened her door. He put his forearm on the roof of the car and leaned in. "You okay?"

She let out a long breath. "I don't know how you do this stuff."

"Practice makes perfect."

"Was that Gus?"

"Yeah. It's nice to see he hasn't lost his touch."

Derek glanced toward the plane to ensure the coast was clear, then held out his hand and helped her out of the car. Suddenly she felt light-headed. When she teetered a little, he wrapped his arm around her waist and pulled her right up next to him.

"Easy there," he said. "Can't have you passing out on me."

She dropped her forehead against his shoulder. "I think I'm going to throw up."

"Nope. Government operatives aren't allowed to throw up. Even temporary ones."

When she lifted her head again, he brushed a loose strand of hair away from her cheek and tucked it behind her ear. "You played it exactly right. The plan went off like clockwork. And Gus will thank you for it. He just might make it to his wedding on time."

She glanced at the plane. It was sleek and black and very expensive-looking, with a Sterling International insignia on the side.

"Sterling International?" she said.

"It's one of the fronts for my team's operation."

Alyssa nodded. Nothing about this stuff surprised her anymore. "What's Gus doing with Teague?"

"Putting him in a room at the back of the plane so he'll never know you're on board."

"Isn't he going to wonder what happened to me?"

"If you see him after all this is over, just tell him you were taken off airport property and released."

"Will he wonder why I didn't call the police?"

"Not after you tell him that we proved to you that we were with the government and swore you to silence about what you had seen. That way you supposedly don't know why we grabbed him in the first place—only that we had the authority to do so."

"And what story will Teague be telling me concerning why he was nabbed by government operatives and then released?"

Derek smiled. "I have no idea. Should be an interesting one to hear, though."

"Okay. So all we have to do now is fly to Houston, break into a building and steal some stuff." She took a deep breath and let it out slowly. "Piece of cake, right?"

"Yep. With your retinas and Teague's key card, we can't miss."

Gus stuck his head out of the plane. "He's secure."

"Preflight done?" Derek asked.

"She's ready to go."

Derek turned to Alyssa. "Speak in a whisper until we get off the ground and there's enough engine noise to cover the sound of your voice."

She nodded.

"Okay. Let's move out."

As soon as they were on board, Derek tossed his suit coat aside and pulled off his tie. Alyssa looked around, marveling at the size of the plane. Six leather-upholstered seats accommodated passengers up front. Glancing toward the back of the plane, she saw a short hallway with a door that led to a small bathroom, and a closed door beyond that.

"Is Teague back there?" she whispered.

"Yeah. It's a room we use for in-flight conferences that doubles as a lockup for prisoners."

Alyssa nodded.

She and Derek belted themselves into their seats. Derek quietly introduced her to Gus, and she liked him immediately. His sandy brown hair, blue eyes and friendly smile made him handsome in that boy-next-door kind of way, in contrast to the dark intensity Derek exuded with every breath. Then she remembered that Gus hadn't looked the least bit friendly when he'd grabbed Teague out of the limo and held a gun to his head. Clearly he had the ability to get serious fast when the situation called for it.

"It's nice of you to do this," Alyssa told him as they taxied down the runway. "Not every man would take time out on his wedding day to help an old friend."

Gus glared at Derek. "Yeah, and that old friend's debt is mounting by the hour."

"Hey, you know I'm loaded," Derek said. "Just name your price."

"You think it's money I want? No way, buddy. One of these days I'm hitting you where it *really* hurts."

His words were barbed but his meaning wasn't, and Alyssa had the distinct feeling that when it came to comparing which man had put himself on the line for the other one the most, he and Derek had lost track of the score a long time ago.

Once they were in the air Derek unbuckled himself and stood. "I'm going to have a talk with Teague," he told Alyssa. "You stay here with Gus. And don't believe a word he tells you. Remember— he's out to get me."

"Just go torture the prisoner, will you?" Gus said. "Alyssa and I will be just fine."

When Alyssa raised an eyebrow, Derek gave her a quick wink. "Don't worry, sweetheart. I might talk him to death, but that's about as violent as things are likely to get."

He disappeared into the back of the plane and closed the door behind him. Alyssa turned to Gus. "So, you're getting married today. That's so exciting."

"Yeah. Assuming all goes well. If not, Derek can kiss his ass goodbye."

"He appreciates this. But you know that, don't you?"

"Yeah, I know." Gus's expression became solemn. "We've been through a lot together. There's not much I wouldn't do for him, and that includes fly a plane to Houston on my wedding day." He sighed dramatically. "I must be out of my mind."

Alyssa smiled. It warmed her heart to know that no matter how much of a loner Derek seemed to be, at least he had one true friend.

"So tell me about the two of you," Gus said.

Her heart skipped. "There's really not much to tell."

Gus glanced over his shoulder, then lowered his voice. "Well, you could start with that week you spent together in Seattle."

Alyssa froze. "Derek told you about that?"

"Oh, yeah. Does that surprise you?"

"Yes, it does."

"It surprises me, too. To tell you the truth, he never talks about the women he's with. Never. But after that week in Seattle…" Gus shook his head. "Good Lord. I thought I was going to have to gag him to get him to shut up."

Alyssa thought back to the days after Derek had left her, how desolate she'd felt, how betrayed. She couldn't believe he'd talked about her the way Gus was describing.

"So how do you feel about Derek?" Gus asked.

The question blindsided her. The whirlwind events of the past day coupled with lack of sleep had pretty much rendered her unable to think straight. *Derek* rendered her unable to think straight.

"I don't know where this is going to go. He's not an easy man to understand. And sometimes he can be a little…difficult."

"Difficult?" Gus made a scoffing noise. "You're even nicer than he said you were. What you really mean is that he can be a pain in the ass."

She smiled. "Occasionally."

"But he's crazy about you, Alyssa. Absolutely, completely, off-the-charts *crazy*. No matter how much crap he dishes out, please don't ever forget that."

She thought about how Derek had told her to

leave last night even as he was praying she wouldn't, and she had to believe that was true.

"He's very focused on his job," she said.

"Yeah. Too focused."

"What do you mean?"

Gus looked over his shoulder again, then back at Alyssa. "He needs out. The sooner the better. Life's passing him by. But the reason he pours everything into the job is that he has nothing else. And since the work he does and the lifestyle he leads keeps him from *having* anything else, it's a treadmill I'm afraid he's going to stay on forever."

Alyssa thought about Derek's apartment. Stark. Barren. More like a hotel room than a home. "He just doesn't know what he's missing."

"No. He doesn't. So will you do me a favor?"

"What's that?"

"Show him."

Alyssa sat back, feeling a tingle of exhilaration at the possibility that there might actually be a future for them.

Show him.

If only she had the first idea how to do that.

WITH TEAGUE CUFFED and belted into a seat at the back of the plane, Derek went through his wallet and instantly recognized the key card to his penthouse apartment. Once again, Teague's predisposition for creating cookie-cutter buildings had made Derek's job easier.

Derek stuck the card into his backpack, then went through the rest of the man's wallet, looking for anything that might tell him whether Teague was up to something else he shouldn't be. As he searched, he occasionally flicked his gaze to Teague to assess his state of mind. Even in the cool air inside the plane, the man was sweating as if he'd run a marathon, which meant he was growing more anxious by the moment. Good. Derek had every intention of using that anxiety to his advantage.

"What's happening here?" Teague said finally. "Where are you taking me?"

"On a little business trip to Houston."

"What happened to Alyssa?"

"The woman? She was escorted out of the airport. You're the one we're interested in."

"She'll call the cops. She'll tell them what's happening."

"No, I don't believe she will."

"Why not?"

"Let's just say she's being taken care of."

Teague looked a little queasy when Derek said that, as if he thought that "taken care of" was a synonym for "snuffed." And if Teague was making that assumption, he was undoubtedly a little uptight about what Derek intended to do with him. That was fine with Derek. No need to relieve him of that fear just yet.

Derek flipped through the rest of the wallet, found nothing of use and tossed it aside. He searched every pocket of the man's soft-sided briefcase, but that netted him nothing, either.

"You can't do this," Teague said. "You can't just—"

"I assure you I can. I'm authorized to do anything

I damn well please with a man who's blackmailing half a dozen U.S. congressmen."

Teague went pale. "I don't know what you're talking about."

"Let's dispense with the denials. Owens talked. He told us that the DVDs are in your apartment safe. Is that true?"

Teague was silent.

"Hmm. This is a problem. When I ask you a question, I expect an answer. Evidently I'm going to have to persuade you that it's in your best interest to talk to me."

"You won't hurt me. If you're with the government, you can't—"

"Let's get something straight here, Teague. I'm not 'with the government.' Think *mercenary*. I work on a contract basis only. And I never promise to follow rules. I only promise to get results."

Teague licked his lips nervously, a rivulet of sweat coursing down his temple.

"Okay," Derek said. "All I want is a simple answer to a simple question. Are the DVDs in the floor safe in your apartment?"

Teague's eyes flicked back and forth as he considered his predicament. Finally he let out a harsh breath of resignation. "Yeah," he said. "They're there."

"Are you lying to me, Teague?"

"No. They're there. I swear to God they are."

This guy was so typical. He was greedy enough to be a blackmailer, but he really didn't have the guts for it. Since he wasn't a professional criminal, a little intimidation went a long way toward coercing him to tell the truth.

"Well," Derek said, "looks as if Owens really did know what he was talking about. What's the combination to the safe?"

Teague told Derek the numbers and he wrote them down.

"Now the PIN number for your key card."

Teague rattled off those numbers.

"What do you think, Teague? Shall we review these numbers? Give you a chance to make corrections to anything you might have accidentally misstated?"

"I told you the right numbers," Teague muttered.

"For your sake," Derek told him with a pointed stare, "you'd better have."

Derek had already committed the numbers to memory, but he stuck the piece of paper into the side pocket of his backpack for future verification if need be.

"Here's what's going to happen," he said. "We're flying to Houston and I'm going to retrieve those DVDs. If you're telling me the truth and they really are there, you'll be in the clear."

"In the clear? What do you mean?"

"You'll walk away. We're not interested in prosecuting you."

Teague's eyes shifted back and forth skeptically. "Yeah, right."

"If we prosecute you, the content of those DVDs has to come out. We don't want that. We only want this whole mess to go away."

"I won't go to jail?"

"That's right. This is your lucky day. You committed a felony offense and you get to go on with life as usual."

"Life as usual? Do you have any idea how much money I'm going to lose when that trade bill passes?"

"You should be counting your blessings that you won't be doing prison time." Derek eyed him menacingly for a long moment. "Now, I want you to listen very carefully, because there's one more thing you have to do."

Teague looked at him warily. "What's that?"

"Sell the Dallas building."

Teague's face flooded with disbelief. "What?"

"You heard me. Sell it."

"The Waterford? I'm not selling that building. The occupancy is ninety-eight percent!"

"I don't care if it's booked from now until the turn of the next century. Sell it. And I don't give a damn who you sell it to. Just as long as you're no longer the owner."

"I can't just suddenly sell it. People will ask questions!"

"Which you don't have to answer. All of your assets are privately held. You call the shots. I want to see it on the market Monday morning at a fire-sale price, because I want it to move quickly. And you're never to set foot on the property again."

"I don't see why—"

"You don't have to see why. You just have to do it."

"And if I don't?"

Derek paused for a moment, then walked over to where Teague sat. Very deliberately, he put his hands on the armrests on either side of his chair and leaned in, skewering him with a fierce stare. "The last man who thought he could get away with ignoring a simple request of mine spent two months in intensive care sucking his meals through a straw. *After* three hours of surgery."

Teague swallowed hard, his face turning chalk-white.

"You can try it if you want to," Derek said. "But rest assured if you don't do as I ask, there'll be a bed in ICU with your name on it. Now, do I make myself clear?"

Teague looked as if he'd swallowed his own tongue. "Yeah," he said, barely able to choke out the word. "Perfectly."

"Monday morning," Derek said as he backed away. "I *will* be watching."

He grabbed his backpack and left the room, shutting the door behind him, then went to the front of the plane.

"Her name is Sally," he heard Gus say. "She's a little crazy, wildly opinionated, unbelievably beautiful—"

"And she'll put up with you," Derek said as he took his seat. He turned to Alyssa. "That's a must-have trait where Gus is concerned."

"I don't know," Alyssa said, smiling at Gus. "I think Sally is a very fortunate woman."

Derek shot Gus a look of exasperation. "I see you've been spewing all kinds of self-aggrandizing propaganda."

"No propaganda here," Gus said. "Every self-aggrandizing word I speak is the gospel truth." He flicked his head toward the back of the plane. "How's our passenger?"

"He verified everything. The DVDs are in the safe."

"How do you know he's telling the truth?" Alyssa asked.

"Experience," Gus said. "Derek knows what he's doing."

"He's too scared to lie," Derek said. "He's not a professional criminal. A little intimidation goes a long way." He turned to Gus. "What's our ETA?"

"We'll touch down in half an hour."

"Okay," Derek said to Alyssa. "Just sit back and enjoy the ride."

WHEN THEY LANDED in Houston, the rental car Derek had arranged to have brought to the plane was there waiting for them. He and Alyssa left Gus with Teague and headed for the Concorde. Houston traffic could be a nightmare, but fortunately, today it was light. He checked his watch. They were right on schedule.

He glanced over at Alyssa and saw her wiping her palms on her pants.

"How are you doing?" he asked her.

"Don't mind telling you I'm a little uptight."

"Good. It'll keep you on your toes."

"Just how far up on my toes am I going to need to be?"

"It's a simple job. Just do exactly what I tell you and everything's going to be fine."

Ten minutes later Derek saw the building in the distance, a carbon copy of the Waterford in Dallas. He pulled into the alley behind the building and they slipped out of the car. Derek threw his backpack over his shoulder and he and Alyssa walked nonchalantly to the parking garage. Before they entered it, though, he saw a man getting out of his car. Derek grabbed Alyssa's arm and whispered to her to wait until the guy made his way through the double doors leading into the first floor of the building.

Once the garage was unoccupied, Derek led her across the garage to the penthouse elevator lobby. She put her face to the retinal scanner and, after a moment, he heard a click.

Perfect.

Derek opened the door and they headed to the elevator. He swiped the key card, punched in the PIN number and the elevator slid open. Moments later they were on their way to the penthouse.

"So far, Teague's information has been right on the money," Derek said.

"What if he gave you the wrong safe combination?"

"I have software that'll break into the safe. It'll just take a little longer."

Alyssa nodded.

"I'm going into the bedroom by myself. I want you to stay by the elevator. I should be gone for two minutes, max. But if something goes wrong, I want you to get the hell out of here."

Her eyes rounded. "What? No. Not without you."

He handed her the keys to the rental car. "If I'm caught for some reason, I don't want you implicated. Get back on this elevator and get out of the building."

"Why didn't we talk about contingency plans before we got here?"

"Because there's only one contingency plan, and it's very simple. And that's for you to get out if things go wrong."

"But—"

"No buts." He gave her a pointed stare and finally she nodded.

The elevator bell rang softly, indicating that they'd reached the penthouse. The doors opened and they both stepped off. Derek held up his palm, silently telling Alyssa to stay put. She nodded. He went down the short hall leading to the living room, then made a quick sweep of the rest of the apartment to make sure they were alone. Once he was back in the living room, he glanced down the hall leading to the elevator and gave Alyssa an "okay" signal. She nodded. Then he pointed to the master bedroom, indicating that he was heading to the safe.

When he flipped back the rug and verified the presence of the floor safe, he was thankful once again that Teague had been a tightwad with architect fees. He punched in the five-digit code and pulled the safe open. Inside he found five folders, all stacked nice and neat.

If all his jobs were this easy, he'd be bored to tears.

Just before he reached for the folders, though, he thought he heard a noise in another part of the penthouse. He stopped and sat motionless, holding his breath, listening.

Nothing.

But still he waited. In the distance he heard the faint rumble of a jet flying overhead, but that was all.

He slowly relaxed, deciding he must have imagined it. After quickly grabbing the folders and stuffing them into his backpack, he shut the safe and flipped the rug back over it.

"Freeze!"

Derek spun around and stood, shocked to find himself looking down the barrel of a gun.

13

WHEN ALYSSA HEARD the shout, she snapped to attention, fear racing through her. That wasn't Derek's voice. Somebody else was in the penthouse. She edged down the short hallway and peered around the corner. From that vantage point, she could see through the living room into the master bedroom.

A security guard was holding a gun on Derek.

Suppressing a gasp, she ducked back around the corner. She hadn't even heard him come in. It was as if he'd been aware of their presence and had approached as silently as possible. But how? How could anyone have known they were here?

"Facedown on the ground!" the guard shouted.

"Hey, man," Derek said, holding up his palms. "Take it easy, okay?"

If something happens, I want you to get the hell out of here.

No. She couldn't do that. She couldn't leave Derek here. She remembered what he'd told her yesterday when she'd accidentally shot out that window. *If I'm caught, nobody in Washington is going to admit I exist. That means that if I'm arrested, they won't do a thing to help me.*

He couldn't go to jail for this. She had to do *something*.

"I said get down on the ground!" the guard shouted again.

As if he had decided to comply, Derek let the backpack slip off his shoulder. He caught it in his hand, then slowly lowered it to the floor, his eyes never leaving the gun in the guard's hand. Alyssa knew instinctively that Derek remained in the game as long as he was still on his feet. But even though he was only a stride away from the guard, it was a stride too far. If only the guard were distracted....

Alyssa looked left then right, spying a vase on a nearby shelf.

Do it.

She grabbed the vase, pausing only a second before hurling it hard across the living room. It crashed into the wall with a clatter of broken glass. The guard spun around. Derek reacted immediately, diving for the hand that was holding the gun.

A shot exploded.

For a split second Alyssa's mind went to the worst possible scenario, but Derek was still on his feet and he managed to catch the guard's wrist. He slammed the man's hand against the wall, dislodging the gun, then spun him around and forced him facedown on the floor. Derek whipped his own gun from the small of his back and pressed it against the guard's neck.

"Put your hands behind your head," Derek said in a voice that left no room for disobedience.

The man complied.

"Don't move a muscle," Derek said. "Not one."

Derek rose, grabbed the guard's gun and shoved it into his backpack, then tossed the pack over his shoulder. Thinking ahead, Alyssa spun around and raced back to the elevator to open the doors. Moments later, Derek was there, too, and the instant he was inside, she jabbed the button. The doors closed and the elevator descended.

She leaned against the wall, her hand clasping her throat. "Somebody had to have heard that shot. Are we going to be able to get out of here?"

"Shouldn't be a problem. They'll lock down the building, thinking that will keep us contained."

"What happened?" Alyssa said. "How did the guard know we were in the penthouse?"

"I don't know. Teague's penthouse must have a silent alarm that's not part of the main system."

"Did you get the DVDs?"

"Yeah. They were all there."

They came to the ground floor. The moment the elevator doors opened, Alyssa heard a loud click.

Security had activated the lockdown.

They hurried to the door. "Let's hope this works," Derek said. He slid the key card between the door and the door frame, then yanked the door handle. It didn't budge. Alyssa slid her hand to her throat. *Oh, God…*

He swept it again and she heard the click.

She let out the breath she'd been holding. Derek swung the door open, took her hand and they walked out of the garage through the passage to the alley and then slipped into the car. The moment he started the engine, they took off.

Alyssa put her hand to her chest, trying to calm the painful beating of her heart. They'd just robbed that penthouse. Or the cops would assume they had, anyway. She glued her gaze to the passenger rear-view mirror, waiting for the wail of sirens she was sure was coming. It wasn't until they'd traveled a few miles without red flashing lights behind them that she began to relax.

"I think we're in the clear," she said.

"What did you think was going to happen? That we'd show up on an episode of *Cops*?"

"God, Derek, don't tease me. I'm already about to be sick."

"Nah. We were a hell of a team. Ever think about becoming a government operative?"

She turned to him. "Are you out of your mind? There's no way I'd—"

That was when she saw the blood.

"My God. Derek, you're bleeding!"

He glanced at his arm. "Don't worry. It's only a flesh wound."

"Were you shot?"

"Yeah, but it's no big deal."

"No! Don't you dare say that. That's what the hero always says in the movies right before he passes out."

Derek grinned. "Trust me, sweetheart. A Band-Aid will fix me right up."

"Are you sure?"

He glanced over at his arm. "Well, maybe one of the giant-size ones."

Alyssa closed her eyes. "I can't believe this is no big deal to you."

"It's what I do. I'm used to it."

Her eyes sprang open again. "Used to getting shot? How many times has that happened?"

"You mean, how many times have I been shot at or how many times have I actually been hit?"

She held up her palm. "Never mind. I don't want to know." She leaned her head against the headrest. "God, Derek, I was scared to death. When I heard that gun go off—"

"When you heard that gun go off, you should have done what I told you to and gotten the hell out of there." He reached over and took her hand, giving her a smile. "But thanks for sticking around."

DEREK GAVE Gus a quick call to tell him they had the DVDs and were heading back to the airport. Alyssa still looked a little shaky, but she was holding it together pretty well considering what they'd been through. He already knew she was bright and beautiful and thoughtful and compassionate. Now he could add *courageous* and *resourceful* to the list.

By the time they reached the plane, Gus had turned Teague loose. The engine was fired up and they were cleared for takeoff. Derek and Alyssa climbed on board and buckled themselves in. Gus taxied to the runway and a minute later they were in the air.

"Mission accomplished," Derek said. "Five congressmen can rest easier tonight. Any problems with Teague?"

"Nope. I turned him loose and he hightailed it out of here. You must have made quite an impression on him. I don't think he's going to be blackmailing any more congressmen anytime soon."

Derek checked his watch. "And look at that, Gus.

It appears we're going to make a certain wedding on time."

"Don't get cocky," Gus said. "Until I'm actually standing at the front of the church, you're not off the hook." Then he glanced at Derek's arm. "Hey, is that blood? What's up with that?"

"He was shot," Alyssa said, still looking a little pale.

"Oh, yeah?"

"There must have been a silent alarm," Derek said. "A security guard paid us a visit before we could get out of the apartment."

"You're supposed to stay out of the line of fire, man. Getting slow in your old age?"

Derek made a scoffing noise. "A miss is as good as a mile."

"A miss? Wrong. If there's blood, it's a hit."

"Nope. You know full well it's a hit only if there's *arterial* bleeding."

"Hey!" Alyssa cried.

They both spun around.

"How can you two joke about this?" She turned to Derek, pointing sharply. "You. Come with me to the bathroom. I'm getting that wound cleaned up."

Alyssa walked toward the back of the plane. Derek looked helplessly at Gus.

"Hey, you've got your orders," Gus said. "Hop to it."

Derek followed her to the tiny bathroom at the back of the plane, where Alyssa had already located the first-aid kit and was pulling out cotton balls and peroxide. She set them on the counter, then told him to take his jacket off. After tossing it on the floor, she examined the wound on his bicep. She closed her eyes for a few seconds, and Derek could tell she felt a little woozy.

"Take it easy," he told her. "It's not deep. There's just a lot of blood."

"It's impossible to tell if it's deep or not until I clean it off. Now, hold still."

She took a washcloth, dipped it in warm water and smoothed the blood off his arm to reveal a crease that was a little deeper than he'd anticipated. It was probably going to leave a hell of a scar, though one more hardly mattered.

"See," he said. "Nothing to worry about."

She dabbed the wound with peroxide. "When we get back to Dallas, you're going to the hospital. I want a doctor to take a look at this."

"Sorry, sweetheart. I have a wedding to go to."

She covered the wound with a large Band-Aid. "Then right afterward."

"That's really not necessary."

"Yes, it is," she said sharply. "You could need antibiotics."

"Nah, I've been hit enough times that I'm bound to have antibodies to every germ in the world."

"Derek, would you just—" Her voice cracked and she turned away.

"Come on, Lys. Take it easy."

"That was a dangerous situation. You were *shot*, for God's sake!"

"Okay, I admit it was dangerous. But I ended up with only a flesh wound. I still don't see why—"

"Because I'm in love with you, damn it, and I don't want to see you hurt!"

Derek was stunned. What had she just said?

Alyssa turned her back to him, her hands shaking as she tried to put the lid on the peroxide. She fumbled with it for several seconds, but she couldn't get the threads to line up. Finally she just set both the lid and bottle down and let out a harsh breath of frustration.

"Okay," she said in a shaky voice, "so it was dumb for me to blurt that out, but there it is. I told you how I feel. But don't worry. I certainly don't expect you to…oh, *hell*."

She tried to move past him, but he took her by the arm and pulled her back.

"Lys—"

"No," she said. "Don't say anything. Please don't. Especially something you'll wish later that you could take back."

The truth was that he didn't know what to say. What to do. He knew he wanted her. Needed her. Was practically obsessed with her.

But love?

He had never let himself get close enough to a woman that she would have a chance to come to care about him, much less fall in love with him, and the very thought of it happening now blew him away. As ignorant as he was about these things, he knew she was offering him something more valuable than gold, but nothing in his life had prepared him for how to deal with it.

Or how to accept it.

He softened his grip on her arm. "I don't know what to say."

"I told you. Please don't say anything."

"You don't understand."

She inched her gaze up to meet his.

"What you just said…" His throat felt so tight he could barely speak. "Nobody has ever said that to me before."

Alyssa blinked with surprise. "Never?"

When he just stared at her, the most profound expression of sadness came over her face and tears shimmered in her eyes.

Tears. He had no clue how to deal with her emotional state. But he did know that for all the lies he'd told her, he had to be truthful with her now. He had to let her know that loving him came with a price she might not want to pay.

"I told you last night," he said. "I've had a hell of a life. I'm not even sure I know what love is. And that's why I'm no good for you."

"I don't believe that."

"Believe it. You and I together…God, Lys. There's no way. No way that I can possibly—"

She put her hands against his chest. He stopped short, standing motionless. She slid one of her palms upward from his chest to the curve of his shoulder, then behind his neck, as she rose on her toes to kiss him. When he felt the first light touch of her lips at the same time her breasts brushed against his chest, everything he knew he should be saying went right out of his head. Such softness. For all the strength he thought he had, this woman was driving him to his knees.

"Just kiss me," she whispered against his lips. "That's all I want. Just kiss me."

With barely a moment's thought, he dropped his

lips to hers, knowing he was leaping headfirst into a hopeless situation but taking the plunge anyway. Instantly she leaned into him, moaning softly in the back of her throat as she rocked against him, her breasts rubbing against his chest and her abdomen pressing into his groin. At the same time, she threaded her fingers through his hair, then gripped it tightly so she could deepen the kiss.

Memories of the past twenty-two hours flooded his mind. He saw her in that penthouse yesterday afternoon, bravely stealing his gun from him. In his bed last night, whispering words that had smoothed the ragged edges of his heart. In Teague's penthouse, saving him from certain disaster.

He'd had a rough life. A fragmented life. Nothing stable. Nothing lasting. This woman was the opposite of all that. She exuded the kind of warmth and permanence that up to now he'd only dreamed about. Everywhere in his life there was a void, she seemed to fill it. How the hell was he going to go on living without her?

She leaned away, her breath hot against his mouth. "I changed my mind."

"What?"

"A kiss isn't all I want."

14

DEREK TOOK ALYSSA by the hand and led her out of the bathroom and into the room at the back of the plane. He shoved his palm against the door to shut it, then flicked the lock.

"How long till we land?" Alyssa asked.

"Long enough," Derek said.

"Gus? Will he wonder—"

"He'll get the picture."

Derek was already pulling his shirt off. When he dragged it across his wound, he winced involuntarily. Alyssa helped him take it off the rest of the way, trying to avoid his bandage, but he didn't give a damn about the pain. He threw his shirt down and they fumbled with the rest of their clothes, tossing them into a haphazard pile on the floor.

Derek wound his arms around her and dragged her next to him, turning the gentle kiss she'd given him before into something hot and hungry. And she was right there with him, leaning into him and kissing him with an urgency that sent a surge of anticipation racing through him.

Breathing hard, he raised his head and stared down at her heavy-lidded eyes so full of passion.

Then he changed the angle of his kiss and dove in again, trailing his hands down her body, caressing her breasts, letting his thumbs play back and forth across her taut nipples.

She felt good. So damned *good.*

"Derek," she said on a hot breath. "Now."

His heart jolted. No. It had to be too soon for her.

He slid his hand down her waist to her hip, then circled around to dip between her legs, only to get a shock. She was already swollen and slippery against his fingers.

Unbelievable.

He knew he was ready for her. Hell, he'd been ready for her since the moment she'd first touched him. But to have her so hot and willing like this, *demanding,* even—

She arched against him. "Derek, I said *now.*"

He got the picture.

Stopping only long enough to grab a condom from his backpack and put it on, he led her to one of the seats and pulled her down to straddle his lap.

Yes, sweetheart, you're right. You're so right. It has to be now.

To his surprise, though, she stopped suddenly, her hands resting against his shoulders. For several long, unbearable moments, the only move she made was to drag one slow, hot, ragged breath after another. She just stared down at him, her blond hair cascading over her shoulders and her green eyes fixed on his. He'd never had a woman look at him like this, as if her world was going to stop if she had to tear her gaze away.

I love you.

If he'd wondered before whether she was serious about that, he wasn't wondering now. He could see it in every move she made, every breath she took. She poised herself over him and with a single downward thrust she took him all the way to the hilt.

Derek groaned with pleasure, staggered by how unbelievably good it felt. She withdrew, then sank down on him again. Holding her hips, he encouraged her to go deeper and faster. He struggled to get air, overwhelmed by the most amazing feeling of needing and wanting, of reveling in the sheer physical pleasure of it as his heart joined with hers.

She plunged down on him, wildly and erratically, and he strained against her, desperate for release. She dipped her head, then lifted it again, her eyes squeezed closed, her breath coming in sharp, needy bursts.

Her next breath was a gasp.

After a split-second pause, she slammed herself down on him, grinding deep, her fingertips digging into his shoulders. And that was all it took to push Derek right over the edge. Pulse after pulse of pure sensation shot through him. Blinding white light seemed to fill his mind, obliterating darkness from every corner.

Then, slowly, steadily, Alyssa collapsed against him. He circled his arms around her and the brilliant burst of sunlight faded into gentle shades of twilight.

They stayed like that for a long time, the heat of their bodies mingling together, their breathing gradually becoming more measured, then settling into unison. The loud hum of the engines was like anesthesia against the rest of the world, making him feel as if the two of them were the only people in existence.

After a minute he shifted her around until she was sitting in his lap, her arm looped behind his neck, her cheek resting against his shoulder. He dipped his head and kissed her, cradling her in his arms, wondering what the hell he'd done so right to have this woman in his life right now.

I love you.

His mind refused to accept those words. Since he'd first grabbed her in that penthouse yesterday afternoon, the emotional intensity between them had only escalated. She may have believed it when she said it, but in the heat of the moment it was easy for something to come out that she'd didn't really mean. Still, just hearing the words…

It seemed impossible that this could be happening. They'd met up again for just one day. In Seattle they'd been together for only one week, though he'd spent the intervening six months thinking about what it had meant. Even when he'd denied it to himself, she'd still always been in his thoughts, and now as they were together like this, it was as if they'd never been apart. He thought about the next time he'd have to leave Dallas—it would come all too soon—and he couldn't bear the thought of long days and nights without her.

Suddenly there was a knock at the door. They both jumped. Then came Gus's voice.

"Derek?"

"Yeah?" Derek replied.

"Sedgewick's on the line."

"Damn," he muttered under his breath. "I need to talk to him."

"Your Washington contact?" Alyssa said.

"Yeah." He turned and called out to Gus. "Give me a minute." He leaned his head against the back of the seat with a weary sigh, then checked his watch. "We'll be landing soon. You'd better get back out front, too."

"Okay. I'll be there in a minute."

They rose from the seat. As Derek began to dress, Alyssa sat again, curling up in the chair, watching him. He knew he needed to say something, but he didn't know what. There was still so much for him to think about. To work through. To wrap his brain around. He felt so blindingly incompetent at making the right words come out of his mouth that he was afraid to say anything.

Later. They could talk later. Once they were back in Dallas, once the wedding was over, there would be plenty of time. Then it would be just the two of them, and by then he hoped he would have a better handle on this. He hoped.

Before he left the room, he glanced back at Alyssa. Her cheeks were flushed pink and her hair was mussed, her green eyes slumberous with satisfaction, and he didn't think he'd ever seen her look more beautiful.

He walked back to her, put his hands on the armrests of the chair and gave her one last kiss. Then he headed to the front of the plane, leaving her wondering, he knew, where they went from here.

ALYSSA DIDN'T get dressed right away. Instead she stayed in the chair for a minute longer, not completely sure her knees would hold her up. She'd had so little sleep last night, and that, along with the tension of completing Derek's mission and the strength-sapping pleasure of making love with him, had rendered every one of her muscles weak and useless.

She'd never expected to feel this way about him. Beneath his tough-as-nails surface beat the heart of a sensitive and vulnerable man, a man she'd fallen in love with. It scared her a little that he seemed so afraid of the prospect of the two of them together, but after last night she knew where that fear came from, so maybe she could counter it. She could love him so much that it would make up for all the times when love had been so absent from his life. She could love him until he felt as if he couldn't live without it.

She could love him until he realized that he loved her, too.

After a few more minutes she rose and put on her clothes, then checked her reflection in the bathroom mirror and groaned out loud. Her hair was a mess and her cheeks had that telltale flush that was going to make Gus raise an eyebrow.

Oh, well. There was nothing she could do about that now. Not that it really mattered. Gus had asked her to show Derek what he was missing, and that was exactly what she was trying to do.

She opened the door and went back to the front of the plane. Derek caught sight of her and stopped his conversation with Gus.

"Get your seat belt on," Derek told her. "We're nearing final approach."

Gus put on his headphones to make contact with the tower, speaking all kinds of pilot terminology that went right over her head. She sat and belted herself in.

"So did you talk to the guy in Washington?"

Derek leaned closer and lowered his voice. "Yeah. I told him we've got the DVDs. But I have a little bad news."

"What?"

"The minute the wedding is over, I have to catch the next flight to Washington. They've got another job for my team."

Disappointment surged inside her. "Where will you be going?"

"I don't know yet. They're going to brief me when I get to Washington."

"I hope it's not dangerous."

"It sounds like something routine. Nothing to worry about."

"How long will you be gone?"

"I don't know." He shrugged. "Probably only a few days." Then he gave her a sexy smile. "I'm hoping for a nice homecoming."

She smiled. "I think that can be arranged."

"I can't wait."

Alyssa felt a shot of euphoria at the idea of seeing him again.

"Do you like weddings?" Derek asked.

"Of course. What woman doesn't like weddings?"

"Then come with us."

"Are you sure that's okay?"

Derek turned around. "Gus! Mind if Alyssa comes to the wedding?"

Still talking to the tower, Gus just gave Derek a thumbs-up.

"See? No problem."

Alyssa smiled. "Okay," she said. "Sounds like fun."

After what the three of them had been through together today, she was looking forward to seeing Gus get married, and she wanted to meet Sally.

But most of all, she thought with a smile, she couldn't wait to see Derek in that tuxedo.

THEY LANDED a few minutes later, and as they were taxiing to the hangar, Derek watched Gus alternate between tapping his fingers nervously against the yoke and checking his watch. Barring anything unforeseen, though, they had time to make it to the church.

Barely.

Still, once they'd reached the hangar, Derek could tell that Gus wasn't holding it together too well. They leaped out of the plane and headed for the limousine they'd left there earlier.

"Come on, you guys," Gus said. "We need to move it."

"Take it easy," Derek said. "The church is only fifteen minutes from here."

"Right. And it's almost eleven-fifteen. We still have to get ready. *Crap*. I wish I could have gotten dressed before we flew to Houston."

"Right. Putting a gun to Teague's head while

you're wearing a tux. Who do you think you are? James Bond?"

They reached the limousine and Gus turned to Derek. "Gimme the keys. I'm driving."

"Like hell. You'll get us stopped for speeding. Then you really won't make it on time."

"I'll take my chances."

Derek opened the driver's door. "Just get in the car."

"After you give me the keys."

"I don't ride with lunatics. Right now, you're certifiable."

"Don't you understand? I'm getting married in forty-five minutes!"

"You're not if you don't get in the damned car!"

With a sharp glare, Gus ripped open the back door of the limo and got inside. Derek rolled his eyes with exasperation. As he and Alyssa got into the front seat, he wondered what had happened to his friend's brain. He had watched Gus in the tightest situations imaginable and the man had barely blinked. But toss one bride his way and suddenly he lost his mind.

A few minutes later they were heading down Mockingbird Lane in the direction of the church, Gus fidgeting in the backseat the whole time. They approached a yellow light, and when Derek brought the limo to a halt, Gus groaned.

"What are you doing? You could have made that light! Do you have any balls at all?"

"Will you shut up? This limo's a block long. The green light barely gives me enough time to get the damned thing through the intersection."

"The second this light changes," Gus said, "and I

mean the very *instant*, I want that gas pedal on the floor. Do you hear me?"

Derek thunked his head against the headrest, then turned to look at Alyssa, who was smiling furtively.

"He's gone insane," Derek muttered.

"I heard that," Gus snapped.

Look out, Derek thought. *This is what love does to a man.*

Still, just thinking about how much Gus was looking forward to marrying the woman he loved and getting on with their life together sent a surge of longing through Derek that he hadn't anticipated. Out of the corner of his eye, he looked at Alyssa, and he thought about how they'd made love not thirty minutes ago. He still felt the aftershocks and, judging from the blush that was still on her cheeks, she felt them, too.

Find a way. Work it out. Whatever you do, do not *let her go.*

"Damn," Gus muttered. "It's eleven-thirty. Sally must be going nuts."

"We're almost at the church."

"I'm going to call her. Let her know we're almost there so she doesn't worry anymore."

"For God's sake, Gus. We're only a few blocks—"

Derek felt Alyssa's hand on his arm. He sighed with resignation.

"Good idea, Gus," he said. "Why don't you give Sally a call?"

As Alyssa sat back with a look of amusement, Gus pulled out his cell phone and hit a few buttons. He waited for a moment, then a grin broke out on his face.

"Hi, baby… No! It's okay. I'm back in Dallas…Yes!

I swear I'll be there on time... Yep. Derek is with me. We can be dressed and ready to go in a few minutes... Yes. Of course I'm sure. Everything's going to be all right. We're getting married, baby. Swear to God." He paused, and another kind of smile came over his face. "Yeah, I've been thinking about tonight, too. A heart-shaped tub, a few bubbles, a little champagne...oh, yeah. I can't wait, either."

Derek rolled his eyes.

"I'll be there in a few minutes..." His expression softened. "I love you, too, baby." Gus made a kissy noise into the phone, hung up and settled back in his seat with a smile of satisfaction.

Derek glanced at Alyssa, shaking his head sadly. "Is he a goner, or what?"

Alyssa smiled. "I think it's sweet."

"Sweet. Uh-huh. Pretty soon he's going to be calling her Poopsie and painting her toenails."

"Right," Gus said. "I'm the crazy one. I get to spend the next two weeks with my wife on a Caribbean island. I'm thinking that beats the hell out of the Nicaraguan jungle where you're spending the next month."

15

DEREK HOPED that somehow Alyssa hadn't heard what Gus had said. But then she turned to the back-seat, blinking with surprise.

"What did you say?"

"I said I'm going to be drinking rum from a coconut and lying in a hammock while he's slapping mosquitoes and dodging bullets, and he thinks *I'm* the fool."

She looked back at Derek. "I thought you said… you're going to *Nicaragua?*"

He swung the limo into the parking lot behind the church, pulled up to the back door and killed the engine. Gus leaned over the seat, his gaze shifting back and forth between them.

"Uh…Derek?" he said. "As always, if I'm supposed to zip my lips about something, you might want to tell me so."

"Too late."

"Sorry, man."

"Just go. I'll be there in a few minutes."

Gus glanced at Alyssa with a look of regret. "Remember what I told you on the plane," he said. "Please."

Derek had no idea what Gus meant by that. He didn't care. All he cared about was finding some way to explain this to Alyssa.

Gus got out of the car and trotted toward the door of the church. Derek watched him go, afraid to turn back, afraid to see that look of betrayal in her eyes.

"I asked only one thing of you," she said, her voice tight. "One thing. And that was to tell me the truth. Always. But what you told me wasn't even close to the truth, was it?"

"What was I supposed to do?" he said suddenly. "You got all worried over a flesh wound. How would you have reacted to my going into a far worse situation than the one we faced today?"

"Not well."

"Then it's best if you don't know."

"I'll never know, will I?"

"What?"

"If you're telling me the truth about anything."

He started to tell her that he'd never lie to her. Not about anything significant. To him, this wasn't. But to her...

It was significant. And it was a lie.

"You told me you'd be gone only a few days. Gus said a month. What's the truth?"

He paused, the tension in the car suddenly so thick he felt as if he were choking. "It'll be at least a month."

She gaped at him. "My God. Were you just going to leave me here waiting for you, thinking you were going to return any day, when you *knew*..." When she faced him again, there were tears in her eyes. "How could you *do* that to me?"

When he didn't respond, she reached for the door handle. "I have to go."

"No. Stay for the wedding. Then we can talk."

"There's nothing to talk about. You're living the life you want to live. The one you're driven to live. Coming and going at a moment's notice, gone for weeks at a time. But being your Dallas stopover is no life for me."

"You make it sound as if there will be other women. That's *not* the way it's going to be."

"Can I really believe that?"

"Yes!"

"You haven't even told me your real name and yet you want to go on as if this is a nice, normal relationship. It's not. It can never be."

"Alyssa—"

"You're never going to let me know you completely. And even if you were willing to do that, what kind of relationship could we hope to have if you show up only once a month for a few days—a week if I'm lucky?"

Derek felt a flood of anguish, because he knew she was right. He was only home three or four days a month. That had never mattered to him before. But now, with Alyssa—

"I'm sorry, Derek," she said. "But I want all of you. Body, heart and soul. Or I don't want you at all."

He felt as if that heart she'd talked about had just fallen through the floor. "Are you telling me that when I come home and I want to see you, you'll tell me no?"

Indecision swept across her face. For a moment

she refused to look at him, staring down at her hands instead. She took in a deep, steadying breath. "Yes," she said firmly. "That's what I'm telling you."

"Fair warning, Lys. Locks don't stop me."

She whipped around. "No. Don't you even *think* it."

"If that's what it takes—"

"Damn it, don't you *dare* show up out of nowhere again!"

"You told me you loved me. Did you mean it?"

Her lips tightened and she looked away again. "Yes."

The word came out as a whisper, and that word held the last shred of hope he had.

"If you love me," he said, "then how can you do this?"

"I didn't do anything," she said quietly. "You did."

Derek felt a stab of regret. She was right. His first inclination had been to lie. To keep what he was doing a secret. He'd told himself it was only because he wanted to spare her the worry of knowing where he was going and what he was doing. But the truth was that he'd just been so solitary for so long that he didn't know how to let somebody else into his life.

Maybe he never would.

She reached for the door handle again and he grabbed her arm. "Alyssa, *please* don't go."

She turned back with an expression he couldn't read. Slowly she reached up and rested her palm against his face. He softened his grip to a caress, hoping she'd relent. *Praying* she'd relent. When she trailed her thumb softly over his cheek, tears clouding her eyes, he was sure she had changed her mind.

"Goodbye, Derek."

No. She couldn't be leaving him. She *couldn't*.

Alyssa dropped her hand to his shoulder, then stroked her finger lightly beside the bandage on his arm.

"Stay safe, okay?"

With that, she got out of the car and shut the door behind her. She circled around the church and disappeared out of sight. Derek had no idea where she was going, but right now it probably didn't matter to her.

As long as it was away from him.

She was gone. Out of his life. And he had the most terrible feeling it would be the last time he'd ever see her again.

ALYSSA WALKED to a restaurant down the street from the church and called a cab, and twenty minutes later she was back at the Waterford. By the time she came into her apartment, she was feeling so tired she headed straight to her bedroom. She'd been up late last night, then risen before dawn this morning. The tension of the trip to Houston had taken its toll—she felt as if every muscle in her body had reached its limit.

But the emotional drain was worse.

She slipped into bed, hoping to put Derek out of her mind and just sleep for a while, but despite how tired she felt, she lay awake, her stomach swirling with disappointment—overwhelming, almost incapacitating disappointment—that nothing had changed, that the man she loved couldn't tell her the truth. Worse, he thought nothing of leaving her for weeks at a time and expecting her to be there when he returned.

Six months ago she'd felt as if she was on the verge of having a relationship with a man that was good and real and lasting. And even afterward, no matter how pathetic it had been, in the back of her mind she'd still held on to a tiny thread of hope that someday he'd be back, that he'd have an explanation for everything that had happened, and then he'd become a man she could build some kind of future with.

She'd gotten two out of three. And that wasn't enough.

She rolled onto her side, tucked her arm beneath her pillow and closed her eyes. But the moment she did, she saw images of foreign countries and flying bullets, and she knew she was going to spend the rest of her life wondering where he was and what he was doing.

And whether he was still alive.

She opened her eyes again and stared at the ceiling, wishing that somehow there was a way to wipe clean every memory she had of Derek and go on with her life as if he had never existed. But she knew that could never happen. If she lived to be a hundred, she was still going to imagine every day that she might look up to see his handsome face in some unlikely place and fall in love with him all over again.

TWENTY MINUTES LATER, Derek stood at the front of the church sanctuary with Gus. They'd entered with the minister through a side door and now they were waiting those few moments before the processional began. Derek glanced around at the flowers and ribbons and pews full of smiling faces, everything lit warmly by noon sunlight streaming through stained-glass windows. It was a day for celebration, and for Gus's sake, Derek intended to keep a smile on his face even if it killed him.

While they were dressing, Gus had asked him what had happened with Alyssa. Derek simply told him it was over. They'd been so rushed that the conversation hadn't gone much further than that, but Gus told him they'd talk later. Derek couldn't imagine what there was for his friend to say. There was only one meaning to the word *over*, and no amount of talking about it was going to change it.

The organist began the processional music. Soon the groomsmen escorted the bridesmaids up the aisle. Then the music changed and Sally appeared at the back door, wearing one of the most dazzling wedding dresses Derek had ever seen. As she came up the aisle, Derek cast a sideways glance at Gus, who was staring at his bride as if she was the light of his life. Sally's father handed her over to Gus. They faced the minister and the service began.

Derek tried to stay upbeat. To focus on Gus and Sally and what this meant for them. But every word the minister spoke made him a little more miserable.

To have and to hold...for better or for worse...the union of husband and wife in heart, body and mind...help and comfort given one another in prosperity and adversity...

Soon the words became a blur inside his mind and all he could think about was Alyssa. About how he'd been so close to true happiness for the first time in his life, only to have it slip away like sand through his fingers.

The minister stared at Derek. Derek stared back.

"The ring," Gus whispered.

"Oh." He reached into his pocket and pulled it out. He handed it to Gus, who put it on Sally's finger, a symbol of his promise to love, honor and cherish her for the rest of their lives.

Finally the ceremony was over and Gus kissed his bride. Looking at the two of them, Derek was struck by the fact that their vows had been more than empty words. They were two people who would love each other forever.

A short time later Derek drove to the hotel where the reception was being held. It was the last place he wanted to be, but he was determined at least to put in an appearance.

In the ballroom sat dozens of round tables covered with white linen tablecloths and extravagant centerpieces. The wedding cake sat on a long table at the front of the room, a stunning five-tiered creation that could probably feed three times the number of people present. Flowers and china and silver and crystal were everywhere. Everyone in the room seemed to be filled with joy, an emotion Derek was sure he would never feel again as long as he lived. Still, when the time came, he managed to slap a smile on his face and make a toast to Gus and Sally, who looked so deliriously happy he wanted to scream.

Derek downed his drink, then headed to the bar for another one. And chances were that on his flight to Washington in a few hours, he'd have another couple for good measure.

He glanced over to see Gus say something to Sally.

She looked at Derek with a sad expression. Gus gave her a quick kiss, then came over to where Derek stood.

"Nice reception," Derek said.

"Yeah, it is, isn't it? But that's not what's really on your mind."

"No," he admitted, "it's not."

"Listen to me, Derek. I watched you and Alyssa together. I know what you had in Seattle. It may have been only one week, but I've never seen you like that about any woman. And now that I've met her, I know what a fool you'd be to let her go."

"Small problem with that. She never wants to see me again."

"How do you feel about her?"

He looked away. "I don't know."

"Then you need to forget about her."

"What?"

"Look, if you don't know how you feel about her, do her a favor and save her the grief of dealing with your stunning inability to make up your mind."

"You're not getting this, Gus. She's already made the decision for both of us."

"Since when do you let other people make your decisions for you? Even the woman you're in love with?"

Derek whipped around. "In love? I'm not—"

"Hell, yes, you are. You wouldn't be so damned miserable if you weren't."

Derek just stared at his friend, wondering if it was possible. The emotion it was built on had been so absent in his life that he wasn't sure he'd ever be able to recognize it, but…

Maybe Gus was right. He'd gone through his

whole life needing no one, only to feel as if he needed Alyssa like he needed air to breathe. That had to mean something, didn't it?

"Even if I am," he told Gus, "I haven't got a clue how to get her back."

"Sure you do. If you go into business with me, you'll be there for her. It isn't as if we haven't discussed it a dozen times."

"You know I can't see myself doing that."

"What's the matter? Can't deal with being an equal partner with me? Do you always have to be the boss?"

"That's crap, and you know it."

"You're right. I do know it. So why don't you tell me what the real problem is?"

"I don't know."

"You're thirty-three years old. You still gonna be doing this mercenary stuff when you're forty? Fifty?"

Derek couldn't see that happening. But he was having a hard time visualizing any alternative.

"I finally figured it out," Gus said, glancing over at Sally, "and it's time you did, too. You can have the job, or you can have a life. You can't have both."

A life.

He loved the sound of those words. And he loved the idea of what came with it. A beautiful, loving woman. Maybe even a family. Someone to come home to. But those things were so foreign that he just couldn't imagine having them.

"I need to think about this," Derek said.

"Yeah. Good move. And while you're off pissing around in some godforsaken country *thinking* about it, some other guy's gonna grab her. Is that what you want?"

Derek blinked with surprise. He hadn't thought about that. He'd just assumed that whenever he happened to come home, she'd be there. But what if she were there in the arms of another man?

"Now, here's what you really do need to think about," Gus said. "Which would you rather do? Spend the next month in a Nicaraguan jungle or here in Dallas with Alyssa?"

All at once Derek felt as if a door had been flung open, allowing him to see into a whole realm he hadn't even realized was there. He'd always had a camaraderie with his team members. A sense of brotherhood with Gus. Those kinds of relationships had sustained him through his entire adult life. But how the hell had he ever reached the conclusion that they were enough?

He had a warm, beautiful, passionate woman who was in love with him. Wouldn't he be a fool to let her go?

"You know all that payback I've been talking about?" Gus said.

"Yeah?"

"There's only one thing you have to do, and your debt's paid."

"What's that?"

"Go get Alyssa."

16

ALYSSA HAD DRIFTED into that hazy world between sleeping and waking, where strange thoughts swirled around in her mind, odd little dream fragments that made no sense at all. So when she heard a noise and awoke with a start, she wondered if it was real or if she'd imagined it. She lifted her head from the pillow and listened.

Nothing.

She lay down again and had just about fallen asleep when she heard something else. Footsteps in her hall?

She jerked her head up again. Yes. She heard footsteps. Somebody was in her apartment.

Sitting up quickly, she pressed her back against the headboard and pulled the covers up to her chest. A man appeared at her doorway. Her heart nearly stopped.

Derek.

He was wearing a tuxedo, the tie hanging loose around his neck. He just stood at the doorway, staring at her.

"My God, Derek! You scared the hell out of me!"

"I'm sorry."

"How did you get into my—" She stopped short. "Oh, hell. What am I saying?"

"I told you a lock wouldn't keep me out."

"And I told you *never* to do that!"

"If I'd called you from downstairs, would you have let me come up?"

"No."

"So I didn't have any choice."

"Yes, you have a choice! You can stop *doing* this to me."

He moved toward her. She held up her palm. "No. Don't."

"Don't what?"

"Don't get near me."

He kept coming, and she felt helpless to do anything about it. Short of calling security, she couldn't stop this man from barging into her life anytime he chose to. And even if she called security this time, what about next time?

But there was a bigger question. Who was she going to call to keep him from leaving her again?

She couldn't deal with this. If she let Derek so much as touch her, she'd be lost all over again, back on that roller coaster of wanting him, needing him, loving him, only to end up watching him walk away again.

"Stop!" she shouted.

Finally he came to a halt.

She still held up her hand as though warding him off. "Don't take another step. Whatever you have to say to me, you say it from right there."

"Stone."

Alyssa shook her head with confusion. "What?"

"That's my last name. Stone."

Alyssa felt a tremor of surprise, but she wasn't about to believe anything he was telling her. "And which alias is that?"

"It's the name I was born with," he said. "And I'll tell you anything else you want to know. Anything."

For a moment she didn't respond. What was he saying? That he was going to be truthful with her? Was that possible? If so—

Then she came to her senses.

"No," she said. "Nothing has changed. You'll still be hopping the globe, getting shot at, and I'll still be hugging home base in Dallas. There's no way—"

"I'm disbanding my team."

Alyssa froze with shock. "What did you say?"

"I'm disbanding my team. Staying in Dallas. Gus has asked me to go into partnership with him."

Alyssa just stared at him, unable to believe what he was telling her.

"Now, there will still be some travel," Derek said. "But rarely at a moment's notice. Most of the business will be in Dallas."

Alyssa gazed at him with suspicion. "I'm not buying this."

"You think I'm lying about what I intend to do?"

"No, I think that somewhere between Gus's wedding and here, you lost your mind."

"Nope. My mind is present and accounted for."

"But I know how you feel about what you do. You're not ready to quit."

"Yeah, Lys, I am." He slid his hands into his pants' pockets, his body heaving with a sigh. "I'm tired of going home alone. I'm tired of not being able to put food in my refrigerator because it'll rot before I'm there to eat it. I'm tired of sitting in generic hotel rooms, unable to remember which city I'm in."

"I can't believe you're serious about this."

"What's my alternative? Should I wait six months and hope I'll burglarize another penthouse suite and happen to run into you before I finally get it through my head what's important?"

Alyssa didn't have a clue what to say to that.

"Just for the sake of argument," he said, "let's assume lightning strikes twice and fate throws us together again. What are my odds that when it does, some more intelligent man hasn't already made you an offer you couldn't refuse? Hell, I'm shocked it hasn't happened already. You think I'm taking that chance a second time?"

Alyssa just blinked.

"There's something I have to tell you," Derek said. "Something I should have already told you."

He started toward her.

"No! Tell me from there."

"I'd really rather be over there when I say this."

"No," she said. "Stay right there. If you come over here, you'll be in this bed in under ten seconds and then we won't be talking anymore. We'll be—"

"I love you."

Alyssa stopped short. "What?"

"I said, I love you."

Those words sent a feeling of pure joy surging through her. Just as quickly, though, she tempered it with a heavy dose of wariness. After all, this was the man who had told her he didn't even know what love was.

"Wait a minute," she said. "I'm not sure you know what you're doing, much less what you're saying."

He shrugged. "Okay. I'll buy that. I mean, God knows I'm no expert on the subject, right?"

"So you've said."

"So maybe you can tell me what it means when I think about getting on a plane and leaving you behind, and I get this really sick feeling in my stomach, as if every second I spend away from you is a second wasted. What do you suppose that is?"

Alyssa's eyes widened with surprise. "I—I don't know."

"When I look ahead to the future, it suddenly seems different to me, because I can't think about tomorrow, or next week, or even the next ten years without thinking about you. Do you happen to know what that means?"

She opened her mouth to speak, but nothing came out.

"When I wake up in the morning, I want you with me. Not just tomorrow morning, or the next morning, but every morning for the rest of my life. And I'm a selfish jerk, because I want the nights, too. I want to come home every night and make love to you until neither one of us can stand *up*. I want to...to..." He stopped short, fumbling for more words. "I want to lock you in this apartment for the rest of your life just to make sure no other man so much as *looks* at you."

When she pulled away a little, he looked at her sheepishly.

"Okay, so that one's a little possessive. But you're going to have to take the bad with the good."

Then he fell silent, just staring at her, his expression now solemn. "You're right, Lys. I haven't got a damned bit of experience with this, so you'll have to tell me." He swallowed hard. "Everything I just said. Is that love?"

Alyssa was so stunned that speech still wouldn't come. Tears did, though. Her eyes filled with them, blurring her vision to the point that Derek looked out of focus, yet still incredibly handsome.

"Yeah," she said breathlessly. "I think it is."

"Thank God. Can I come over there now?"

"Yes," she said on a sigh. "And *please* hurry."

He was across the room in an instant, sitting on the bed beside her and taking her in his arms. The unthinkable had actually happened. He really was here and he really had just said he loved her.

"Tell me I haven't screwed this up," Derek said, holding her so tightly he was practically smothering her. "Tell me you love me."

"I love you."

"Say it again."

"I love you. Anytime you need to hear it, just let me know."

"You're going to get sick of saying it, then."

"Never."

He held her for a long time, rocking her gently, kissing her lips, her cheek, her forehead and then hugging her some more. She melted into him, her heart beating crazily with the knowledge that finally, *finally* he was here to stay.

Then he stiffened.

"What?" she asked.

He pulled away and gave her a once-over. "Do you always sleep naked?"

"Uh-huh."

His mouth eased into a broad smile. "I like that."

She put her palm against the satin lapel of his coat, sizing him up, as well. "You look fabulous in a tuxedo."

"Thank you."

"Take it off."

She didn't have to ask twice.

A few moments later Derek slid beneath the covers with Alyssa and when he tucked her into his arms and she rested her head against his chest, she swore she'd never felt more contented in her life.

"So how was Gus's wedding?" she asked.

Derek shrugged. "Nice, I guess."

"What did the bridesmaids' dresses look like?"

"I don't know."

"What color were they?"

He paused. "Couldn't tell you that, either."

"Was Sally a beautiful bride?"

"Yeah, I guess so."

"What color was her dress?"

"Color?" Derek paused. "Aren't they all white?"

"Sometimes they're ivory. Or candlelight."

"Really?"

"Men," she said with mock disgust. "They pay absolutely no attention to the most important stuff."

Derek rolled Alyssa onto her back. Propped on one elbow, he swept her hair away from her forehead, then leaned in and gave her a gentle kiss.

"I haven't got a clue about any of that, sweetheart," he said with a smile. "Because the only woman I could think about was you."

ON MONDAY MORNING, Alyssa went to work in a gloomy mood, disheartened by what she had to do. She'd never written a letter of resignation before, and to have to do it to give up a job she loved was the biggest letdown of all. But just as she'd dragged herself to her computer and turned it on, the building manager gave her the most startling news.

Lawrence Teague had put the Waterford up for sale.

And when Alyssa heard the price, she was flabbergasted. It was his most profitable building, one that was quickly becoming a landmark on the north Dallas skyline, and he was selling it? No, not selling it. Practically *giving* it away. At the price he was asking, she knew he'd have a buyer in no time.

By the end of the day, he did.

Apparently there were still some details to be worked out, but an offer had been made and Teague had accepted it. At the very least, she'd always thought the man had a solid head for business, but dumping the Waterford at a fire-sale price seemed to be one of the more brainless things a businessman could do, and the fact that he'd received an offer by the end of the day only emphasized his sudden lapse in judgment. She guessed there were always real-estate entrepreneurs with deep pockets ready to leap on hot deals, and this deal had been very hot indeed.

The truth was, though, that Alyssa didn't care why he'd done it. She was just excited that he had. This meant she could keep her job. And her apartment. All she had to do was impress the new owner, and she could stay here forever.

She couldn't wait to tell Derek.

When she got home that evening, though, she couldn't fight the momentary twinge of apprehension she felt as she stuck her key in the lock, the feeling that she was going to open the door to an empty apartment.

Derek was sitting on the sofa reading the paper.

When he turned and gave her a big smile, any last remnants of concern she had that he might disappear again were obliterated once and for all.

"Hi, there," he said.

She tossed her jacket across the back of the sofa and leaned over it to give him a quick kiss. "This is nice."

"What?"

"Seeing you here when I come home."

"Yeah. The key was much appreciated. Relying on my computer hacker to get me through the doors in this building was getting a little tiresome."

She came around to sit next to him, unable to contain her excitement any longer. "You'll never guess what happened today."

"What?"

"Teague put the Waterford up for sale."

"He did?"

"Yeah."

"Hmm. Imagine that."

"And he priced it so cheaply that he already has a buyer."

"Well. That's interesting."

Derek turned his attention back to his newspaper. Alyssa looked at him with confusion. She'd expected him to be as shocked as she had been, or at least a little curious about the details. But he was reading the paper as if the sports page was far more fascinating.

"Derek, don't you understand? This means I can stay here. Keep my job. My apartment. This is *big* news."

"I know. I'm happy for you, sweetheart."

But he wasn't acting happy for her, and it was driving her crazy. Then the slightest hint of a self-satisfied smile tugged at the corners of his mouth.

What was he up to?

"Derek?"

"Yes?"

"Did you already know Teague sold the building?"

"Now that you mention it, I think I did hear something about that."

"How?"

He shrugged. "Word gets around."

"You didn't…you didn't have anything to *do* with it, did you?"

He dropped the newspaper to his lap, his brow furrowed in thought. "You know, Teague and I did have a conversation about the Waterford. It kind of amazed me that a big-shot real-estate mogul like him would take advice from a dumb government operative like me, but damned if he didn't."

She couldn't believe it. Somehow Derek had made this happen. She'd been certain she was going to have to quit her job. Give up her apartment. But now, because of what he'd done…

Alyssa plucked the newspaper from his hands, tossed it to the coffee table, wrapped her arms around his neck and kissed him. It was a great big I-love-you kiss that went on so long that Guinness should have been standing by, waiting for them to break the world record.

When she finally pulled away, Derek sucked in a deep breath of total satisfaction. "Wow, Lys. If I'd known all I had to do to get a kiss like that was persuade a blackmailer to sell a high-rise, I'd have done it a long time ago."

"I don't know what you did to make that happen," she said, "and I'm not sure I *want* to know, but…" Her throat tightened with emotion and she had to wait a moment before she could speak without crying. "Thank you."

He smiled. "Now, as far as anyone else knows, I didn't have a thing to do with it."

"Don't worry. Your secret is safe with me." She rested her head on his shoulder with a contented sigh. "Now all I have to do is make a good impression on the new owner so he'll want to keep me."

"I don't think I'd worry too much about that. The new owner is going to love you."

"What makes you so sure?"

"Because he already does."

Several seconds passed before the meaning of his words struck Alyssa. She raised her head and stared at him with utter disbelief.

"You? *You* bought this building?"

"I told you I've got more money than I know what to do with. Now I have something to do with it."

"But even at that price, how could you afford it?"

"Gus and I are in partnership now. In more ways than one. He's fronting the deal. Teague will never know I'm involved."

Alyssa could barely speak for the happiness she felt. "I don't believe this."

"Hey, just because Teague can't be prosecuted doesn't mean he can't be punished. Besides, it's a good investment. Did you know the occupancy is ninety-eight percent?"

"No. You didn't do it to punish Teague. And you didn't do it because it's such a great investment." She laid her head on his shoulder, stroking his chest, loving the feeling of his warm, strong body next to hers. "You did it because you love me."

God, yes, he did. More with every minute that passed.

"Tell me again," he said.

She pulled away and looked at him, her lips easing into a warm smile. "I love you."

Her voice was low and hushed and full of emotion, speaking words he couldn't have fathomed hearing only a few short days ago. Words of commitment. Of obligation. Words that promised a future together. This woman he'd dreamed about for the past six months was in his arms now, telling him she loved him.

No. That wasn't right. He'd dreamed about her far longer than that, long before he'd ever met her. Now he wondered if that was why he'd felt so drawn to her the first time he'd laid eyes on her in that Seattle club. It was as if he had recognized something in her, something he'd desperately needed that only she could give him.

As Derek glanced around this apartment, he felt as if he was seeing things clearly for the first time. Where he'd come from. What he'd become. And most of all, what life could offer. And it was so much more than he'd ever dreamed possible—a woman who loved him and a place to call home.

ALEC MESSINA stared into his uncle Sergio's face and knocked the guy clear into last year with an uppercut.

Okay, so it wasn't really Uncle Sergio but a heavy bag in the rec center gym. Alec's Thursday afternoon self-defense students seemed appropriately impressed with the swing as they whistled and cheered until some punk in the back gave a loud snort.

"C'mon, Perez," the local kid shouted using Alec's assumed name. "What good does it do to throw a punch when every kid here is armed? Even my grandma packs heat."

"Yeah? Too bad Grandma will never have time to draw her weapon if she's facing an opponent with quicker reflexes." Alec was only too happy to mix it up with the punk in the back. "How about a volunteer to help me demonstrate?"

Alec willed him to step up to plate. He wasn't real happy when a throaty feminine voice piped up instead.

"I'm game."

A pathway cleared through his students to give him a clear view of the speaker. Tall, lean and dressed head-to-toe in black, the woman was new to the class. New to Alec's eyes. And holy hell, what a visual treat she made. Long, dark hair twined into a braid that trailed over her shoulder. Utterly straight posture and a kind of catlike grace in her bearing made Alec think some sort of superheroine had swooped into his rec center to test his skills.

"By all means." He gestured to the mat alongside him. "Thanks for offering, Ms.—"

"Torres. Vanessa Torres." She walked toward him with smooth efficiency and none of the rump-shaking strut some women employed to distract men. "My pleasure."

"I'm sure the pleasure is mutual." He eyed her across the distance she left between them. He couldn't catch her scent, which only made him want to get closer. Much closer. "Care to tell me what you're doing here?"

"Just trying to fill some gaps in my knowledge." She smiled as she rolled up her sleeves. "That's okay with you, Mr.—"

"Perez." The false name barely stuck in his throat. Damn, but he wanted to reclaim his life. And he'd like to spend a little time indulging more personal wants.

A very particular hunger sprang to mind as he stared at Ms. Torres and her cool-as-you-please dark gaze. A snort of laughter made Alec realize he'd stared too long.

"Why don't we make like you're going for your gun," he explained, lining himself up with Vanessa. "And we'll demonstrate how quick reflexes can even the odds."

Nodding, Vanessa reached into her jacket as if pulling a weapon.

Alec gripped her arm, stabilizing the hand an attacker might have used to draw a weapon. That left her other hand free, which she promptly used to jab him in the gut.

What the hell?

Morphing out of exhibition mode, Alec refused to let this woman get the drop on him. Lowering his shoulder, he used brute force to lift her off her feet and plow her to the mat.

His next view of her was her flat on her back. A damn fine position for her, if he did say so himself.

Too bad he couldn't enjoy it nearly long enough. She kicked his legs out from underneath him, toppling him.

"Hell." If he hadn't possessed quick reflexes, Ms. Torres probably would have ended up with his shoulder planted between her breasts when he fell. Bracketing her arms with his palms to the mat, Alec held his weight off her as he stared down into assessing brown eyes.

"Lesson number one, don't expect your opponent to fight fair." Vanessa whispered the words between them, but Alec had no doubt the whole class heard.

He'd bet his personal jet that the demonstrations had never been this interesting before.

Clearing his throat, he lowered his voice. "And lesson number two, self-defense is more fun than it looks."

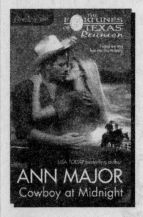

If you enjoyed what you just read,
then we've got an offer you can't resist!

Take 2 bestselling love stories FREE!

Plus get a FREE surprise gift!

Coming in June 2005
from Silhouette Desire

Emilie Rose's

SCANDALOUS PASSION

(Silhouette Desire #1660)

Phoebe Drew feared intimate photos of her and her first love, Carter Jones, would jeopardize her grandfather's political career. So she went to Carter for help finding them. But digging up the past also uncovered long-hidden passion, leaving Phoebe to wonder if falling for Carter again would prove to be her most scandalous decision.

***Available at your
favorite retail outlet.***

HARLEQUIN®
Temptation

It's hot...and out of control!

Don't miss these bold and ultrasexy books!

BUILDING A BAD BOY by Colleen Collins
Harlequin Temptation #1016
March 2005

WARM & WILLING by Kate Hoffmann
Harlequin Temptation #1017
April 2005

HER LAST TEMPTATION by Leslie Kelly
Harlequin Temptation #1028
June 2005

Look for these books at your favorite retail outlet.

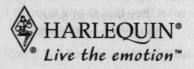

HARLEQUIN®
Live the emotion™

www.eHarlequin.com   HTHEAT

Silhouette® Desire®

presents the next book in

Maureen Child's

miniseries

THREE WAY WAGER

*The Reilly triplets bet they could go
ninety days without sex. Hmm.*

WHATEVER
REILLY WANTS...

(Silhouette Desire #1658)
Available June 2005

All Connor Reilly had to do to win his no-sex-
for-ninety days bet was spend time with the
one woman who wouldn't tempt him. Yet
Emma Jacobsen had other plans, plans that
involved a *very* short skirt and a change
in attitude. Emma's transformation had
Connor forgetting about his wager—but
was what they had strong enough to last
more than ninety days?

Available at your favorite retail outlet.

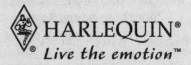